STARTING A DREAM

In Life And Love

Glenn A Bateman

Dedication

In Love and Memory of My Three Angels

Neil, Bo, and Scott

Gone, but not Forgotten

STARTING A DREAM

In Life And Love

Chapter 1

"The future belongs to those who believe in the beauty of their dreams."

Eleanor Roosevelt

There were light snow flurries falling from the night sky and settling on an already frozen ground in this Midwestern community. The snow covered the area, including the overflow parking that surrounded the Wheatley High School gymnasium. Inside the gym, the biggest wrestling match of the season was taking place.

The crowd noise was deafening on the inside. Both teams were undefeated, and this mid-February contest was the last dual match of the season. Most of the crowd was on their feet as the two heavyweights were squaring off in the last individual match of the evening.

I was pacing the sidelines, as I often do while coaching, and shouting out encouragement to my Junior heavyweight Buster Smythe. My name is Mickey Cassman, head wrestling coach of the visiting Troy High School. My Dad named me Mickey after his favorite New York Yankee, Mickey Mantle. Obviously, Mick's number 7 became my lucky number.

We were in a rivalry that has lasted for many years, with Wheatley winning the championship the last four years. This is my fourth year as Troy's Head Wrestling Coach. I have tried to build the program over the years, working with the elementary and middle school boys referred to as a feeder program. Many of these young men have now worked their way onto the varsity and junior varsity teams. We have yet to beat the powerhouse Wheatley team since I have been the coach.

Today's team score, however, is tied 23-23 going into the last individual match of the night. Buster is a big strong, and sturdy heavyweight who has gotten better every year. Buster also played offensive and defensive tackle on the varsity football team. His agility and quickness made him second-team all-league in football.

Buster's opponent was Wheatley's senior heavyweight. Jalen Bennett. Both boys were undefeated.

There are 30 seconds left in the match. Both boys are on their feet, sweat covering their entire bodies. Both are exhausted. Jalen leads the match 4-3, and if he could just hang on, he would win the match. Wheatley would be the league champion for a fifth straight year.

As I pace, I cup my hands around my mouth and yell to Buster, "look for that opening, Buster!" Buster and I have been working in practice on using his quickness. Everyone knows that towards the end of a match, wrestlers get tired and start to lean on their opponent and sometimes get careless.

"When he reaches," I yell. That means Jalen normally reaches for Buster's head with his right arm and will try to hold on and run out the clock. Buster could use his quickness and push the arm up and use a "duck under" maneuver to get behind Jalen. He will then attempt to bring him down to the mat for a 2-point takedown.

With 16 seconds remaining, Jalen reaches for Buster's head with his right arm. Buster instinctively pushes the arm up with his left hand, and using his quickness, he ducks his entire body under the arm and gets behind Jalen.

The entire gym is on its feet. Buster needs to bring Jalen down to the mat, under control, to secure a 2-point takedown. Buster bearhugs Jalen. With all his veins showing in his neck, arms, and legs, he lifts Jalen off his feet. Buster brings Jalen down to the mat and lands on top of him.

The referee points to Buster and holds two fingers in the air indicating a 2-point takedown, and now Buster leads 5-4! Both sides of the gym are yelling for Jalen to get up and for Buster to hold him down. Jalen, however, has run out of steam and can barely move under Buster's grip and his weight.

The Troy crowd and teammates count down 3-2-1! It is over. Troy has finally defeated Wheatley by a score of 26-23 and won the league championship!

Chapter 2

Buster helps Jalen up, and both boys shake hands and hug. The referee raises Buster's arm, indicating him as the winner.

Buster runs over to the opposing coach to shake his hand. I greet Jalen with a handshake and tell him how great a match that was. I like this sportsmanship tradition that our league uses.

Buster comes running over to our side with both arms and fists in the air. Buster jumps into my arms for a big hug, nearly knocking me over.

Pandemonium sets in. The team gets behind me and picks me up on their shoulders. The Troy loyal fan base is lined around the mat, cheering like crazy. The school had chartered a bus to allow the student body to attend. Parents were in tears. Some of the dads had wrestled for Troy, and some had never beaten Wheatley.

The Wheatley coaches and wrestlers, as well as the home crowd, were very respectful and filed out quietly. They realized that they had witnessed two powerhouse wrestling teams battle to the final second. They were disappointed but entertained and respectful.

I could feel my emotions on sort of a high. Being on top of the wrestlers' shoulders, feeling the respect of these young men. Wrestling is a long winter sport, and it takes many hours of practice and grueling workouts. I cannot even count the number of hours I invested in the season. The same goes for my assistant coach, Andy.

Looking over the entire gym, with my open collar, my tie halfway down, and my sleeves rolled up two turns, my eyes begin to water. My emotional side just could not hold back as I reached down to shake each of my teammate's hands.

Chapter 3

It was quite a bus ride back to our home school. The cheering and joy were refreshing, and it gave me time to relax. The seniors in the back of the bus were leading cheers. One of the seniors yelled out to Buster, "I've never seen you move that quick, Buster, unless it was to the lunch table."

Buster yelled back, "maybe someday when you grow up, little guy, you will be this big as well." The lighter weights and heavier weights always enjoyed busting on each other. Everyone laughed. The comradery and closeness of this team were outstanding.

When we got back to the school, the wrestlers were still handshaking, hugging, and slapping each other on the backs. The varsity wrestlers still have the end-of-season tournaments, divisional and sectionals, which could qualify them for the state tournament. The junior varsity season was over, and many of them started clearing out their lockers.

I walked into my office, turned the lights on, and realized that my evening was far from over. I sat at my desk and started doing my end-of-the-match paperwork. I usually write a summary and send it to the local paper, the Troy Times. There was a sports reporter at the match who interviewed me after, so that was one less thing I had to do. I wrote an announcement for the morning announcements. The wrestlers like hearing their names over the announcements in homeroom.

As the wrestlers were filing out, they would peek into my office and say, "good night, Coach Cass." Most of my colleagues called me Cass or Mick. The students called me Coach Cass or Mr. Cassman. I am a high school physical education teacher. I get to know all the students in the school. I enjoy the rapport that I have with the students. I really enjoy the close bond that I have with the wrestlers.

I logged into my computer and entered the stats for the evening. I keep track of individual and team scoring. The boys like looking at those at the end of the year, hoping they improved from previous years. I smile and look at where the team improved. Andy, my assistant coach, came into the office to grab his coat and told me he and his wife were going out for a drink. Would I like to join them?

"You know Andy," I said. "I think I will just head home, relax, and reflect on my own. But thanks anyway, and say hello to Diane for me."

"Okay," Andy replied, "but you need to get out more. You are alone too much since…."

I put my hand up in a stop position. Two years ago, my fiancée, Mary, was killed in an auto accident, hit by a drunk driver. I cried and grieved and still miss her companionship. I miss the things we used to share. The fun we used to have. I buried myself in my work. I am an assistant football coach in the fall, working with the stats, taping ankles, and wrists, scouting other teams, and just about anything to help the coaches. Then I pour myself full-time into the wrestling program. It keeps me busy, and I try not to think about Mary and what life would be like with her. I still have not mastered that part of the grieving process. "Say no more. I appreciate the concern; however, I just want to relax tonight. You guys go have a good time and have a drink for me. Great job this year, Andy; you are a wonderful coach and a good friend. You and Diane enjoy the evening. Tip one for me, my friend."

As I watched Andy leave the office, I thought that he would be an outstanding head coach someday.

As I was finishing up and straightening my desk, I heard that the showers were still on. I was concerned that the wrestlers had left the showers on. I decided to go turn them off. As I came around the corner, I saw the seniors were still in the showers.

"You guys going to camp out here all night?" I asked.

Gary, one of the captains, spoke for the group. "Cass, we do not want to leave. This is our last dual match together, and we want to soak up the memories." I smiled, and my emotional side brought tears to my eyes.

"I'm going to miss you guys," I said. "We have been together for 4 years, and look what we accomplished together. You guys will do great in whatever you do in life." I always preached to the athletes that high school sports, especially individual sports like wrestling, will teach them lifelong lessons. "Just make sure you guys get out of the shower before you turn 30," I joked.

Chapter 4

After everyone left, I said goodbye to Joe, the night custodian, who was prepared to lock everything up for the night. "Have a great evening Cass," Joe said. "Great match tonight, and congrats on the championship. Be careful driving because it is icy out there."

"Thank you, Joe," as I shook his hand. "Thanks for all you do." I always try to show my appreciation for those who work hard and sometimes do not get recognition. Joe smiled, and I felt like I had made his night. "You be careful yourself and get home safely to your lovely wife."

I walked to the parking lot and unlocked my 1983 Ford Mustang GLX, V8 Convertible, red with a white top. The car brought back many memories with Mary. We picked the car out together. In the summer, we would put the top down and take long rides up in the mountains and along the lakes. We laughed a lot, especially when I was teaching her to learn the 4-speed stick shift on the floor. There were lots of herkie jerky starts and lots of laughs.

It would be a long time before I could part with that car and that part of my life. I also own a jeep, which I should be driving in this weather.

The ride through the community of Troy was relaxing. It was a still winter evening. Snow had stopped falling as it glistened on the ground. The snow crunched under my tires. The stillness of the night was peaceful.

It was a 20-minute ride to my house. I live at 44 Syracuse Lane, which is a 2-bedroom, 2-bath ranch, all red brick with white trim and white shutters. This was supposed to be our starter home. It was very homey and comfy for Mary and me. We would spend many nights by our wood-burning fireplace during the winter. We had plans to expand the home, including thinking about a future nursery for a future Cassman!

My life changed after Mary's death. My first thoughts were self-reflection. I had spent so much time teaching and coaching and possibly not enough time with Mary. I blamed myself for not giving more attention to "us." Mary never complained about my work. She was very supportive and attended every event. Still, if I had spent more time with her? I keep coming back to those same thoughts. I was not too proud to seek the help of a therapist, Dr. Helen Morgan, who helped me get through some of the tough times. Dr. Morgan said, "people never stop grieving." Then she added, "time and changes in your life help your mind to better deal with grief."

I have donated a significant amount of money to programs geared towards trying to correct the drinking and driving issue in the state, including the local chapter of AA. I have been a guest speaker at some of their meetings. I have traveled around the state speaking about drinking and driving. I hope that I can save one life at a time. One grieving family at a time.

As I hang up my coat and kick off my shoes, I go straight to the fireplace. I throw in some kindling and some smaller logs and flick the starter to start the fire.

I go into the kitchen and start looking for leftovers. I like to cook, but my schedule does not allow much time for me in the kitchen. I find a leftover casserole of sausage and mac n cheese. I put the dish in the microwave. I grab a beer and open the top.

I am not a big drinker, maybe more when I was younger. Sometimes I will relax with a beer or two or a glass of white wine.

The microwave beeps. I put a significant amount of the casserole on a plate. Grab a napkin, fork, salt and pepper, and my beer and head to the fireplace. I set my dinner on the coffee table and stare into the fireplace. So many memories with Mary come back to me. Drinking wine by the fire. Talking about that evening's wrestling match. Talking about the wrestlers. Mary was my biggest supporter. I miss her terribly.

I look at the fireplace mantle and study our framed pictures. The happy times. The loving times. There was no TV tonight. Just eating my dinner in silence. Just reflecting.

Chapter 5

The remainder of the season was anticlimactic compared to the exciting championship match with Wheatley. The end-of-the-year tournaments, the divisional and sectional rounds, yielded some place winners for our team. None of the wrestlers qualified for the State Tournament. The season came to an end.

There was our end-of-the-year banquet, which was sponsored by our parents' booster club. I was asked to MC the event. I told a few jokes, summarized the season, and gave out awards, all sponsored by the booster club.

The end of the season meant it was time to work with the elementary and junior high wrestlers and help the football team in the weight room. It was also a time to relax some.

My parents had retired to Florida. Easter recess was approaching, so I decided to fly down to see my folks, Wally and Ruthie. I could relax on the beach, ride in their golf cart, and just enjoy the time off. I am not much of a golfer, but it felt good to be out in the sunshine and "try" to hit the ball straight. I have an older brother, William, who lives with his wife, Martha, in New England. I am 32, and William is 39. We do not see each other as often as I would like.

When I got back from Easter break, I was summoned to the administrative office to meet with Assistant Superintendent Bill Handley. One of Bill's responsibilities is to provide personnel for the entire County school system.

The meeting was at 9:00 am, but I like to be early, so I arrived at 8:45. I always feel that being on time is considered late, so I try to be early for appointments. His secretary, Mabel, who has been with the school system for 30-plus years, smiled when I came through the door. "Good morning, Coach Cass," she said. Mabel's grandson is part of my wrestling program. "Congratulations on the Championship."

"Thank you," I replied. "You look mighty attractive today." Mabel blushed and waved a hand in my direction. She reached for the intercom and announced to Bill Handley that I was there.

"Send him right in, Mabel," I heard on the intercom. Mabel smiled and said, "Mr. Handley is ready for you, Coach."

"Thanks, Mabel," I replied.

As I entered the room, I noticed a group of people seated around a table, which made me a bit nervous. Besides Assistant Superintendent Bill Handley, there was my Principal, Paul Horton, my Athletic Director, Eddie Sampleton, and a man and woman that I did not recognize.

I stood at the door, wondering what was happening and why I was summoned to this meeting. Bill stood up and broke the ice by offering his hand, "thank you, Coach Cassman, for coming this morning." He motioned to a chair with his other hand. "Please have a seat at the head of the table." Bill noticed the anticipation in my movements. "Don't worry, Coach, we have something we would like to share with you, and we think it's a good thing."

All eyes were on me for my reaction. I just smiled and nodded to the group. "As you are probably aware," Bill started. "Our Troy school's enrollment has decreased significantly over the years." I was not sure where this was going. I have only been teaching at the school for 4 years. Being the last person in seniority in the physical education department, I always worried about being laid off. Was I going to lose my job? How could this be a good thing?

"We are being forced to make some changes," Bill continued. "We have decided to move you to a different school." The schools in the County are controlled by one central administrative office. Seniority rules govern teachers throughout the entire County, which encompasses 3 school districts. So even though I do not have seniority in my current school district, I can be moved within the county to another school district.

Thoughts are flying through my head, teaching, coaching wrestling, assisting the football program, and my colleagues. I nervously said, "Okay," with a quizzical voice.

"Coach, next school year, we are assigning you to the Mayville School District." Bill continued. Mayville was a nice little village located in the lower-income section of the county. People in Mayville tend to stay there through generations. "We have discussed the wonderful job you have done with the wrestling program at Troy," Bill continued. "Athletic Director Sampleton has agreed to move your assistant coach, Andy, to the head coaching position at Troy. You will become the new head coach of wrestling at Mayville. The program needs a shot in the arm."

A "shot in the arm" was an understatement. Mayville was at the bottom of the league standings and had only won a few matches over the past 4 years that I recall. On the other hand, I felt good for Andy, who deserved the head coaching opportunity and would do well at Troy.

Bill introduced Karen Fryer, the principal of Mayville. Then he introduced Larry Bagwell, the Athletic Director. "At Mayville, we have much younger teachers in the PE department," Bill went on. "So, this will put you in a better position as far as seniority."

My mind started to spin with thoughts going in all different directions. Going to a new school, leaving the wrestlers that I have worked with for the past 4 years, and rebuilding a wrestling program at Mayville. There was silence in the room as the group waited for my reaction. I finally turned to Mrs. Fryer and Mr. Bagwell, who were seated to my right. "It would be my pleasure to work for you two at Mayville High School," I said with a smile. "I look forward to meeting the students at your school and welcome the challenge of rebuilding the wrestling program."

Karen Fryer, who was closest to me, stood up to shake my hand. "Welcome to the team, Coach Cassman," she said. Larry Bagwell stood and walked around Karen's chair to shake my hand. He put a hand on my shoulder and offered his assistance in any way that he could. He asked me if I would assist with the football program, doing scouting, taping, and weight training as I did at Troy. "It would be my pleasure, Mr. Bagwell."

"Larry," he corrected me. My parents had brought me up to address my elders or bosses as Mr. and Mrs.

"And it's Karen," said the principal.

The meeting was wrapped up cordially, and I thanked them for the opportunity. As I left, I gave Mabel a nice wink, which elicited another blush. I told her to have a great day and walked out the door.

I had so many thoughts; I did not lose my job due to declining enrollment. I was really going to miss the closeness I had with my wrestlers. On the other hand, it was kind of exciting to try to rebuild a struggling wrestling program at Mayville. I was starting to look forward to this new chapter in my life.

Chapter 6

After the Easter break, the school year winds down quickly. News of my transfer reverberated around the school. I always felt accomplished by the respect that I seemed to garner from my students. I tried to treat all the students fairly, athlete or not.

I did not allow bullying or hazing in the locker room or in the gym area. It did not matter what type of ability the student had. I wanted them to feel included in the physical education program.

Of course, the wrestlers were like sons to me. The sport of wrestling taxes a person's mind, whether it be motivational or thinking of the next move to make. As a coach, I tried to sync my mind with theirs. I wrestled in high school and college, so I knew what they were going through.

Wrestling is physically and mentally draining. There are three 2-minute periods in high school wrestling. The third period becomes a challenge. Sometimes the body says no, but the mind tries to say yes. Sweat is pouring into your eyes. Your opponent is physically trying to control you. This is one of the times that the wrestler reaches down for that "something" that we, as humans, possess in order to win the match.

Wrestlers were coming into my office daily just to chat. I knew they were trying to let me know how important I was in their lives. It was a great feeling.

As the school year moved into exam week, there were plenty of hugs and some tears. I wish the underclassmen good luck in the upcoming season, "but not when you wrestle against Mayville," I joke. I told them that Coach Andy could do a great job. "I will follow you guys in the paper," I tell them.

The senior wrestlers were going in different directions; college, military, and the workforce. I told them that the four years of wrestling would give them a good foundation for what they will experience in life.

After the final exams and graduation, I cleared out my office. After I boxed everything up, I sat at my desk one more time. It was time to reflect. This job, this office, this school had been my refuge after the terrible loss of Mary. It was my escape. It was like my second home.

The administration told me to take as much personal leave time as I needed when Mary was killed. I came back to my job sooner than most expected. Everything and everybody connected with teaching and coaching served as an escape for me.

My eyes started to water. I dried them with the back of my hand. I smiled. The smile was partially because of the memories of the past four years. The smile was also of the challenge ahead at Mayville High School.

I picked up my last box, threw the strap of my laptop bag over my shoulder, turned out the lights, and headed out. No regrets.

Chapter 7

The end of June, July, and early August usually serve as "vacations" for me. I have a cabin up in the mountains, about 2 hours away from my home. I hop into my jeep, load up with supplies, and head off to the mountains.

As I drive, so many thoughts are going through my head. The past four years, the future at Mayville, and of course, the many times I took this drive with Mary. The cabin was always a place to clear my head and just enjoy the outdoors. The windows are down, and the fresh spring air feels great.

When I got to the winding dirt road leading to the cabin, the trees were in full bloom. The birds are singing. It is a beautiful June day.

I park my jeep in front of the cabin. I walk up the stone steps and notice that I need to do some raking of leaves and debris. That is going to be relaxing.

I open the cabin and hang up my keys on the hook by the door. I go directly to the windows and open them wide. It needs a little airing out.

After carrying in my supplies and putting the perishables in the refrigerator, I walk outside to check out the scene.

My backyard has a beautiful view of the lake behind. I look over the land and notice my fire pit must be cleaned out. There have been many cookouts in that pit.

I go to the shed and pull out my canoe and oars. I drag them down to the water. I hang up my hammock between two very old but sturdy oak trees.

All my fishing gear is stored in the shed. I check the poles and lines to see if anything needs to be replaced. I would gather some bait in the morning and probably go out fishing tomorrow.

Mary and I used to call this place heaven. I guess it seems more like heaven when you have someone to share life's serene pleasures with.

My summer consists of canoeing, fishing, and cooking in the fire pit. I would relax in the Adirondack chairs off the back porch. Spend some time in the hammock, reading.

Most mornings, I can be seen paddling out to the middle of the lake and casting my line. Before I leave the shore, I carefully prepare all my gear; tackle box, cooler with plenty of water, a PFD (personal flotation device), and a first aid kit. I do not bring my cell phone because I wish to escape from the rest of the world. I do not use any advanced technology, like a fish finder. I am "in one" with nature and the fish.

I like to anchor where the fish "tell me." I see the beautiful fish jumping out of the water, so free and happy. My life is free and happy. I have a wonderful and supportive family. I enjoy my profession. I enjoy life's beauty, which is why Mary and I wanted to spend time in nature at our cabin.

People ask about my future, about a partner. I am content to be a teacher, coach, and motivator of young men. Since I lost Mary, my family, my job, and nature are my partners.

Oh, I have a bite. He is a fighter but looks small. After I reel him in, I talk to him and send him back to his family. Most of my fishing is "catch and release." It is about the sport. It is about relaxation and reflection. One can get lost in thought out on the lake.

Later in the morning, I catch a beautiful 18-inch redfish. It was a challenge bringing him in. First, I drag the line until he gets caught. I pull the rod up, then reel rapidly while dropping the tip down.

After scooping him into my net, I set him in my bucket. Looks like dinner will be yummy! I will wait until I get to shore to prepare the catch.

When I finally get to shore, I take precautions scaling the catch. I use gloves, goggles, and plenty of newspaper to collect the scales. The scaler is a handy tool to have in your tackle box. I gut and trim the fish. I take the trim pieces back to the lake and feed the fish, who are waiting for their meal. There is no waste.

Cooking my fileted redfish in the fire pit sends a wonderful smell throughout the area. I already prepared my baked potato. I cut open the potato and fill it with butter, onion, cheese, and some herbs.

Then I wrap the potato tightly with aluminum foil and throw it in the fire.

I eat my fish and baked potato, along with a cold beer, outside. The redfish has a sweet, mild unique flavor. I listen to all the critters singing and "talking" to me. This is a part of life that is relaxing and enjoyable. I may even toss a morsel to a nearby critter as I talk to him.

The lake community comes alive in the summer. My cabin is isolated but close to the center of a small town. Local churches like to have outdoor bazaars, carnivals, and lawn fetes. There are fruit and vegetable stands everywhere you turn.

Sometimes I will walk into town and just walk around and marvel at how these folks live a simple life in a small town. It is a town where everyone knows your name. If you walk into Walter's Country Store, him and his wife, Edna, will greet you and wish you well when you leave. If, for some reason, you forgot your wallet or purse, they will just put it on your tab, and you pay the next time you come in. That is rare today.

The town has parades in the summer, especially on the 4th of July. The Veterans have a big presence in the community. I have a great deal of respect for Veterans.

I roam by the little league field and watch the young boys and girls jumping up and down, enjoying their team's success. I watch the parents and grandparents in the stands, cheering and encouraging. I noticed that families from the previous game had taken their picnic baskets to the adjacent park and were having a nice picnic.

There's very little stress in this small community. They seem far away from the outside world and the outside world's problems. It is very heart-warming and relaxing.

I smile when I notice an elderly couple walking together, holding hands. How cute! I am so happy for them. I wonder what my life will look like when I reach that golden age. I believe that if I live my life right, there will be a plan for me. I believe there is a plan for everyone. Sometimes those plans have interesting twists and turns in them. I am interested in what is planned for me around the next turn!

Chapter 8

My cabin has two bedrooms and one and a half baths. The larger bedroom has a queen bed in it. The smaller bedroom is part sleeping and the other part an office. I spent a little time in the office going over the Mayville football playbook that the head coach sent to me. I like to familiarize myself with their system so that I am available to help wherever needed. I also try to sketch out practice schedules for the wrestling program.

Wrestling season does not start until the first week in November. However, some of the wrestlers usually like to get a jump on the season and do some training in the weight room and on the track.

All this paperwork is relaxing for me. I sometimes work on it in the morning with a cup of coffee or in the evening. Most mornings, however, I am out on the lake.

I have a small television in the cabin, which I rarely use. I prefer to enjoy nature, its beauty, and its sounds. My favorite bird is the male cardinal; such beauty. One of my favorite sounds is that of the owls. I had planted numerous jasmine bushes around the property.

The jasmine scent from the white flower that blooms in the spring, is one of my favorites! Another of my favorites are the beautiful smelling gardenia bushes on my property.

Sometimes I can get a New York Yankees baseball game. I will set up the TV outside and grab a beer and try to enjoy the game.

At night I sit in the Adirondack chair and watch the sunset over the lake. What a beautiful sight. I like to sit after the sun sets and watch the reddish-orange glow across the horizon. I think that God had a plan for these sunsets and the beauty that they give us.

I had a science teacher in high school talk about sunsets. He said, "think how many sunsets you will see for the rest of your life." Of course, as a high school student, I did not really appreciate the importance of that saying. I am 32 now, and I am starting to wonder how many more sunsets will I see in my life. How many more beautiful glows in the sky will I witness?

Too many people drive by sunsets and their afterglow without appreciating the beauty of it all. If they are not outside, they may be inside watching television, on their cellphone, or playing a video game. Nature is a gift that we all need to appreciate.

Those are my thoughts as I watch the reddish-orange glow spread across the horizon. Summer breaks can be relaxing and thought-provoking. It can also prepare me for the upcoming new school year and all its challenges.

During the school year, I try to stick to schedules and deadlines. I try to have a plan for everything. During the summer, there are no schedules, no deadlines. There are no plans.

By the middle of August, I am relaxed and ready to move into a new chapter in my life.

Chapter 9

The middle of August is when football practice starts. I pack up my jeep and head back into town. I park in front of my home on Syracuse Lane. I unlock the house and start unpacking my jeep. I pull my jeep to the far side of the driveway and open the garage door. It is time to rev up the mustang, put the top down, and head to town.

Tonight, would be a good night to make a nice dinner since tomorrow will start double sessions in football. I rarely have time to make a big dinner. My life usually consists of fast food and frozen meals. Tonight, I plan to make garlic creamed chicken with rice and green beans. I will make enough to have leftovers for a few days. Leftovers are another one of my delicacies.

I try to go to bed early because of early football practice. Because of the summer heat, the first session is early. I have trouble sleeping, which is normal.

After a few short hours of sleep, I get up at 5 am. After coffee, a bowl of cereal, and orange juice, I am ready to go.

I arrive at the school with the anticipation of meeting a new group of young men. The head football coach, Charlie Quinn, has been with the school for over 20 years. He introduced me to the players. I had researched their roster and knew that there were a few wrestlers on the team.

The first one who came over to welcome me was their senior captain, Neil Ellis. Neil is the epitome of a stud. Neil is 5 ft. 9, 180 solid pounds. He has muscles on top of muscles. Neil is a good-looking boy with blonde hair and blue eyes. "Welcome, Coach Cassman," Neil said as he offered his hand.

"Call me Cass if you like. I am pretty much known by that name," I said as I smiled and shook his hand and felt the grip. I figured that I would let them know my nickname up front.

"Then Cass it is. Welcome." He replied. Neil is a power running back, rumored to run through tacklers and not around them. He is also a linebacker on defense. It is also rumored that he walks around school with a girl on each arm. Neil has a good heart and steps in if other students start picking on the students who cannot protect themselves. Last year as a junior, Neil was one of the captains of the wrestling team.

"I look forward to wrestling season, Cass," Neil surprisingly said. During the past couple of wrestling seasons, the team was coached by two part-time teachers who knew nothing about the sport. There were no other candidates for the coaching jobs, so they took on the challenge. Mayville did not win many wrestling matches. They had some good wrestlers, and Neil was one of them. There was never enough interest in the program, so they did not have enough wrestlers to fill out their roster. They would forfeit weight classes to the other teams, giving up 6 team points every time that happened. "I know you did a great job at Troy," he smiled.

"I can't wait, myself," I said. "Thanks." The excitement was building already.

Another player who came up to me was junior running back Gage Alan. Gage was 5' 6" and 140 pounds. He is also a wrestler, well accomplished. "Welcome, Coach," Gage said. Gage is an excellent student. He plans to pursue some type of science in college. "Neil and I were just talking the other day about wrestling," he continued.

"We are glad you came to Mayville and look forward to wrestling for you." Gage also has blonde hair and blue eyes and is well-built. He is a solid 140 pounds.

"That sounds great," I replied. "I plan to have a meeting right after school starts in September for anyone interested in wrestling. You and Neil can spread the word. The more guys we get out for the team, the better chance we have of filling all the weight classes." Gage knew from last year what I was talking about.

"Sounds like a plan," he said. "Neil and I were already talking it up with some of the guys." The excitement was building and building.

Chapter 10

The school year started the Wednesday after Labor Day. I waited until the following week to hold a meeting. I coordinated with Coach Quinn so that any football players who wanted to attend would be able to come.

Principal Fryer made an announcement a couple of days in advance. Students could let their parents know that they would be home later because of a meeting with the new wrestling coach.

I set up the meeting in the cafeteria. I was surprised that about 40-plus students showed up for the meeting. Not everyone would join. Some wanted to just listen to what I had to say. Neil and Gage sat up front.

"Welcome," I begin, using my gym teacher's voice. "Thanks for coming. My name is Coach Cassman. I am usually known as Cass. I know you are here because you are interested in wrestling or you just want to see what the new guy looks like." There were a few smiles, but all eyes were on me.

"I'm not going to lie to you," I continued. "Wrestling is not an easy sport to train for. I will train you hard and prepare you for your opponent. Because when you step onto that wrestling mat, you are on your own. It is my job to have you ready for that challenge. When other students walk home after school to play their video games, you will walk down to the wrestling room for practice. We will enjoy holidays with our families but also come to practice during some of those days." All eyes were open and directed at me. A few guys walked in late, but no one paid attention to them.

"I believe in teaching proper technique," I continued. "I also believe in repetition, which means we will spend hours drilling the moves repeatedly. You will find that when you are in a match, these moves will become more automatic. I will never ask you to do something that I did not do when I wrestled. I will also be in my practice gear every day and get right in there with you and demonstrate."

I did not want to stretch this meeting out and lose their interest, so I concluded. "I am asking anyone interested to fill out this form that I passed out at the beginning. I need your name, grade, homeroom number, parents' names, and what weight class you will be looking to wrestle. Stop into my office during gym class and check your weight periodically. There is a scale that I have set aside just for wrestlers. My office door will always be open to you if you need anything or just need to chat."

"One more thing," I wanted to add. "The only thing that I can guarantee is that your hard work will bring you rewards during the season. We will be a team united. We will also have fun. Thanks for coming."

I wanted the students to know that wrestling is not an easy sport to train for, but it elicits many rewards. I think I got my point across. After the meeting, some left right away, but there was lots of mulling around. That is a good sign. Wrestlers come in all shapes and sizes. A coach is always looking for the smaller kids to fill out the lighter-weight classes, as well as the heavier kids and everyone in between.

Neil and Gage were already going around and telling guys that they should try for this weight class and that weight class. There was a boy named Jazz, who I saw in gym class the other day. He always goes around with earbuds in, and teachers are constantly asking him to take them out. He was grooving to his music. Last year the team did not have a heavyweight, so Neil talked one of the football players into coming to the meeting. His name was Bubby Chance. Bubby was big but overweight. He was shy in school and could use something to identify with. Wrestling could be good for him.

Neil and Gage were among the last to leave, and they both looked at me and smiled while giving me a thumbs-up sign. I nodded and smiled back, and waved.

The excitement for all of us was building.

Chapter 11

During September and October, the wrestlers would stop in to check their weight. They would mark their weight on the chart that I made and posted on the wall. Some new boys, who did not attend the meeting, signed up and began checking their weight.

I kept looking at the weights, looking to fill all the weight classes. There were a couple of candidates for the 105-pound weight class. Bo Bennett wrestled last year in the 98 lb. class. He weighs 106, so he was a perfect candidate to fill in for the 105 lb. class. A wrestler must be at the weight class or under to be eligible to wrestle in that class. In other words, for Bo to wrestle in the 105 lb. class, he must weigh 105 or under. He will lose that pound during practice. Some coaches try to starve their wrestlers so they get down to a weight class. I do not adhere to that as a coach.

There was no one signed up for the lowest weight class, 98 pounds. If we did not find anyone, the team would forfeit and give up 6 points every single time. Gage has a freshman brother, who I had an eye on. His name is Scott. Scott lost his right leg to cancer when he was 9 years old. He survived and became cancer free. Scott grew into a happy young man. He is a good-looking boy and gets along great with the other kids. He is also starting to fill out well, like his brother Gage.

I would watch Scott during gym class. As much as he wants to be included in all the sports, he would have trouble with soccer and flag football, to mention a few of the sports. In swim class, he takes his leg off and swims like a fish. He tries his best at most of the running sports. With his lack of mobility, he seems to become very withdrawn.

The next time Gage came to gym class, I invited him into my office. "Have a seat Gage," I started.

"What's up, Cass," he said as he sat, wondering what this was all about.

"Your brother, Scott," I started. "He seems very athletic. I watch him in gym class, and he seems to catch on to all the sports."

"Scott follows all the pro athletes and tries to emulate them. He loves sports," Gage said.

"I hope this comes across the right way," I continued. "I have been looking for someone to compete in the 98 lb. weight class. Do you think Scott would be interested in wrestling? I have witnessed many wrestlers who wrestle on one leg. I predict that with his artificial leg removed, he would weigh about 98 lbs."

"Oh my God, Cass," Gage's eyes seemed to light up. "Scotty would follow me in wrestling and talk about wrestling all the time. No one has ever mentioned that he should give it a try. He would love the opportunity."

"Why don't you talk to him and your parents tonight," I said. "I have him tomorrow for 3rd period. If he is interested, he can sign up and check his weight. Even if he does not fit into the lowest weight class, I would love to have him on the team."

"I'm going to see him after school," Gage said excitedly. This may be the first time that they could be on the same school team together. "Thanks, Coach," Gage said as he left the office.

After my last class of the afternoon, I finished up my paperwork and got my plans ready for the next day. I was ready to change into my football practice clothes when there was a knock on my office door.

I turned around to find Scott Alan standing there. "Coach, can I weigh in?" He asked.

I had a surprised look on my face. My mouth was open. Then I smiled. "Help yourself, Scotty."

Scott went to the area where the scale was. He removed his artificial leg and stepped on the scale, using the wall as balance. The scale read 95 pounds. Scott carefully stepped off, and before putting his leg back on, he said, "where is that sign-up sheet." His smile covered his entire face.

"Welcome to the team, Scott Alan," I said with my biggest smile in a long time. My heart felt full.

There was one important ingredient missing. No one had stepped forward to apply for the assistant coaching position. During my work with the football staff, one of the coaches stood out to me. His name was Pete Donaldson. Pete was in his late forties. He played football and wrestled for 4 years in high school. He went on to junior college and played football.

Pete was very good with the players; they all liked him. He was the backfield coach, so he coached Neil and Gage, fullback and tailback. Pete also had a large family to support. The extra coaching paycheck could come in handy for him and his wife, Suzie. They have 5 children. They kept trying until they had a boy. The kids are all 2 years apart. Kaeli is 12, Maris is 10, Sophia is 8, Emma is 6, and finally, Pete Jr. is 4.

Being out with the coaches, after a few beers, they would bust on Pete. They would say things like, "Hey Pete, don't buy too many beers because you have to save your money for prom dresses and weddings." Another one, especially after a few more beers and referring to Pete Jr, "Hey Pete, how's your little peter."

Pete is a high school math teacher. He had helped me with some of the statistics I was keeping for the football team. We had a good working relationship. One day in October, I approached Pete after football practice. "Pete, you got a minute to chat?" I asked.

"Sure, Cass. What's up, buddy?" He replied.

"I was wondering if you would be interested in being my assistant wrestling coach during the winter season?" I got right to the point.

Pete looked up at the ceiling. I had no idea what he was thinking. He pursed his lips and seemed deep in thought. "Cass, the thought briefly crossed my mind. But, you know, with Suzie and the kids, the holidays." He did not say no.

"I just sprang this on you," I spoke. "Why don't you go home and discuss it with Suzie and your kids? You would be a great addition to the staff. I know Neil and Gage would be thrilled."

There was silence for a long fifteen seconds. "Okay, we will have a family meeting. I will let you know as soon as possible. Thanks for thinking of me."

"Whatever is best for you and your family, I will support you," I said. "Take your time and let me know as soon as you can. If it does not work for you, I must keep searching for a qualified candidate. Thanks for at least considering it."

We both got up and shook hands.

A couple of days later, Pete approached me in my office. "Cass, we had a family meeting. Suzie surprised me and was all in. Her brother wrestled in high school, and she loved the sport. The girls are ecstatic, getting to see all the wrestlers." He rolled his eyes. "Little

Petey wants to join your junior wrestling program. So yes, I am all in. I will talk to Mr. Bagwell later this afternoon and apply."

I stood up and came around my desk, and we gave each other a handshake and a man hug. "Welcome to the team, Coach Donaldson."

Chapter 12

November 1st is the official start of wrestling season in our state. I always joke with my wrestlers that the first day of wrestling season should be a holiday!

The wrestling room was packed with 40+ kids. There are 12 weight classes for varsity. I explained to the wrestlers that wrestling coaches do not pick the lineup. There are what we call "wrestle-offs." All the kids in the weight class wrestle against each other, and the winner is the varsity wrestler.

It is one of the few varsity sports where the coach does not determine or pick the starting lineup. The wrestlers must earn their spot on the varsity. Apparently, this did not occur in the past few years at Mayville.

After the 12 varsity wrestlers are determined, the rest of the boys are part of the junior varsity team. We all practice together and learn the same thing. If a varsity wrestler gets hurt or is sick, the next wrestler in line moves up to varsity.

I have always told my wrestlers that everyone on the team is important. It does not matter if you are varsity or junior varsity or just starting out. Everyone is treated the same. No one gets special treatment. No one is exempt from the duties, like moving mats or washing the mats.

The wrestlers see me mop the mats many times. We use a special kind of disinfectant to prevent skin disease. They also see me moving mats with them. I never ask them to do anything that I will not do. The wrestlers seem to respect that.

I wanted to name captains early. Captains can help enforce some of my policies. I look for captains as leaders. Someone who the teammates look up to or approach with concern. It is not a popularity contest.

After the first week, I asked the team to vote for two captains. I was very pleased when the overall votes went to Neil and Gage. Two excellent captains.

Scotty is fitting right in and really catching on. His sparring partner is Bo, the 105-pounder. They push each other hard in practice and are making each other better.

After one of the practices, I saw Gage talking sort of privately with Leo Carter, one of the 112-pound wrestlers. I called Gage into my office. "What's up, Cass?" He asked.

"Is there something going on with Leo?" I inquired. "Is there something I can help with?"

"Things are a bit tight at Leo's home, Coach," he replied. "The family has two kids in college, and they cannot afford wrestling shoes. I gave him an old pair of mine that I outgrew. They are a bit worn, but they should last for a bit."

"That's great, Gage." I thought for a minute. "What size does he take?"

"Size 7 ½"

"Thanks," I said. "Good work."

I went on to the Amazon website. I ordered a pair of 7 ½ sent to my house. You have to love Amazon and one-day shipping.

Two days later, Leo opened his locker, and he found a new pair of wrestling shoes. His mouth stayed open for a long time. He brought the shoes to my office. "Cass, did you do this?"

I looked around from left to right. "I think the wrestling fairy left them."

"Please thank the wrestling fairy for me when you see him next," he said. He walked away with an extra bounce in his step.

Chapter 13

Early on, I approached Principal Fryer and Athletic Director Bagwell regarding the academic eligibility rules for the athletes. I asked that if I came in early every day, could I set up a study hour in the cafeteria for all the athletes? I argued that with the demand on their time, athletes might need extra time in the morning to complete a homework assignment. They could also be tutored by another student who was more versed in that subject.

The program took off. I would bring my coffee into the cafeteria at 6 am every morning. Athletes from all teams would come at their leisure. It was extended to the entire student body. Sometimes a teacher and student would plan to meet during that hour for extra help. It was quickly named "Cass hour!"

One of my wrestlers, Tycz Brock, was having trouble in all his courses. He attended Cass hour every day but was still struggling in class. His grades were dropping. One morning I had him bring his book to me so I could help him with his homework assignment.

Tycz had a history assignment due that day, and he was having trouble with the worksheet. I looked at his textbook and the worksheet and said, "If you read this chapter here, all the answers are in that chapter. Why don't you read it to yourself and see if you can complete the worksheet."

Tycz looked at the first page for some time. He looked at me and turned the page. After a while, he looked at me with tears in his eyes.

"What's wrong, Tycz?" I asked. Tycz looked down and was silent for a couple of minutes.

"Coach, I…..I can't….." he started.

"Can't what, Tycz," I asked. "You can tell me."

He looked up and said, "I can't read!"

I was shocked. Tycz was a sophomore in high school, and no one had taken the time to realize that his troubles academically were related to the fact that he could not read. No one had ever given it a thought and recommended him for a remedial reading program. He had just been passed along through the system. I put a hand on his shoulder. "Look, Tycz, I am going to talk to someone today. I am going to see that you get the reading help that you need, even if I must do it myself. This is not on you. Don't you dare feel embarrassed or shut down. We will get it fixed. Why don't you go back to your seat and do what you can."

Tycz thanked me and returned to his table. I was livid. How could something like this happen to this poor child? How many adults in the school system looked the other way and passed him on? How many other students have been in the same situation?

I had an early planning period, and I messaged the principal that I needed to meet with her and the head of guidance asap regarding a student.

The appointment was made during my morning planning period. When I got to Mrs. Fryer's office, I was still quite upset. I took a deep breath and told myself to act respectful.

When I was ushered into her office by her secretary, she stood up and said, "Hey, Mick, come on in and have a seat." The head of guidance, Paul Zuke, was there. There was also another woman in the meeting.

"Coach, you know Zuke," pointing to the guidance counselor. "Since your message said it involved a student, I thought I would invite Alice Dillon from the administration office," she said as she motioned to the other woman seated next to Paul. Paul Zuke was wearing black dress pants, a white shirt with a black tie, and a dark blue blazer. His shirt collar was unbuttoned at the neck, and his tie was partially down. What hair he had left was graying on the side. He sported a dark mustache. Paul was in his early 50's.

Alice Dillon looked like someone out of a fashion magazine. Her brown hair was short but perfectly formed. She wore a blue dress that fit her trim figure perfectly. Her heels were a darker shade of blue and were open at the toes, showing her perfectly manicured toenails. Her jewelry was very complimentary. If I had to guess her age, I would guess her about mid-forties.

I was both shocked and thankful that the principal realized that the issue was serious enough to call this meeting. "Thank you for everyone getting together on such short notice." I started and wanted to get right to the point. "It has come to my attention that one of our 10th-grade students is struggling in class because he cannot read. I mean, he literally cannot read."

Alice raised her eyebrows, and Paul sat up straight. Karen sat with her mouth open. I continued while I had the floor. "Look, I am not trying to lay blame here, but this poor student needs remedial reading. He cannot complete his worksheets or homework assignments because he literally cannot read." I decided to be a little bolder. "Regardless of where this student fell through the cracks, he needs special help in reading immediately."

The elephant in the room was the fact that I never said his name, and they were all looking at each other, wondering who passed the buck. No one wanted to ask his name and confess that they had no idea who had the problem.

I made it easy for them. "His name is Tycz Brock. He is in tenth grade. He needs help immediately. He is ready to shut down because he cannot keep up with the class. He is putting the blame on himself, and that can be toxic."

Alice spoke up first. "Coach Cassman, this is going to get my immediate attention. I am embarrassed for the school district that we let this slide this long. I am authorizing immediate testing along with remediation for Tycz." She turned to the head of guidance, "Paul, please speak to all of his teachers and get me a report by tomorrow morning." She turned to the principal. "Karen, we need the remedial reading teacher assigned to Tycz asap, if not sooner." I liked this woman. She got up from her chair and walked over to me. "Coach Cassman, thank you for bringing this to our attention. Keep up the good work."

I got out of my seat and shook her hand. "Thank you, Ms. Dillon."

"Please call me Alice," she smiled.

Chapter 14

During the third week of practice, one of my senior wrestlers, Jake Grayson, stayed after practice to talk to me. Jake was in the 155 lb. weight class and was doing well at practice. I did notice that something was on his mind during today's practice, so I closed my door because it seemed like a personal issue.

"Cass," he started slowly. "I may have to quit the team," he said in a sobering voice like he was ready to tear up. Jake has wrestled for the past four years. This is his senior year.

"What's up, Jake?" I leaned forward with my arms on my desk. "Anything you tell me will be kept in confidence if that works for you."

"My Dad just lost his job at the factory because of cutbacks. My Mom cannot get a job. We have younger kids at home." Jake sniffed to hold back the tears. "The holidays are coming up, Thanksgiving and Christmas. I might have to get a job to help support the family. My dad might get called back to work after the first of the year, but we need help before that. Being the oldest, I feel it is my responsibility to step up and help the family."

I took a moment to let Jake collect himself. It took a lot for him to even come and open up to me. "Jake," I looked him in the eye. When his eyes caught mine, I said, "I have a couple of ideas. Give me a couple of days to come up with some things. Give me a chance to reach out to some groups that can help. Can you do that?"

Jake nodded, "I can do that, Cass. Thanks for listening."

"Just keep that head up high," I said. "You are a good person. Good things happen to good people."

Jake folded his lips together to hold back the tears. He nodded and left my office.

I immediately went to a folder I kept in my drawer. The folder contains lists of agencies that help people in the Grayson family situation. I have so many ideas floating in my head, but I also want to protect the privacy of Jake's family.

I looked up from the folder and stared at the wall straight ahead. When I was growing up, my family went to church every Sunday. We attended Sunday School every week. Went through confirmation and then started taking communion. My family is Protestant. Around the time Mary was killed, my neighbors also lost their 7-year-old son to cancer. That made me question. Not question God, but just question. I was taught that God has a plan. I questioned that if God has a plan, how does the death of Mary or my 7-year-old neighbor's child fit into that plan? Since that time, I have stopped going to church. I never stopped believing or praying. I pray all the time to Mary. My church used to have programs for helping families like Jake's. Should I call them?

I looked down at the folder again. Then I folded it up and placed it in my messenger bag. I threw the strap of the bag over my shoulder and headed home. I had work to do to help this family.

Chapter 15

When I got home, I pulled out one of my gourmet leftovers. I sat there looking at it. Before I heated it up, I decided to call one of the women from my former church. I called Doris Klossman.

Doris answered on the third ring. "Hello." Doris had a very cheery voice and almost sang "Hello."

"Doris, this is Mickey Cassman. Do you remember me?" I was hoping she would forgive me for stopping to attend church.

"Mickey, what a surprise." Doris was always so cheerful. "We were just discussing you and your family the other day. How are Wally and Ruthie? We miss them so, especially your mom's tuna noodle casserole."

"Mom and Dad are doing great. Living the good life in Florida." My parents were on all different committees at the church and always helped. My mom sang in the choir. My dad was the head of the ushers. "Listen, Doris, I know we haven't talked in a long time, and I haven't attended faithfully….."

She interrupted me. "Mickey honey, you do not need to apologize to me or anyone. After the terrible tragedy with that beautiful Mary, we were all heartbroken. Everyone must deal with what life gives them in their own way. Just remember, that the good Lord will not give you more than you can bear. We miss seeing you, honey, but we all understand."

She helped break the ice and made me feel better. "Doris, I am teaching over in Mayville now. The reason I am calling is that I just became aware of a family in need. The father lost his job. The mom cannot find work, and they have two small kids at home besides having a high school senior. The senior wants to quit sports so he can support his family. I know you folks use to have programs set up for just these types of situations, and I was wondering…."

Again, she cut me off. "Mickey, I remember your mom and dad spearheaded a group who brought casseroles over to my house when my Lester died of a heart attack. We had enough food for a year," she laughed. "Your dad even came over and mowed our lawn. Now it is time we pay it forward, son. Give me the family's information, and we will make sure they have a plentiful Thanksgiving."

"Doris, you are a sweetheart," I said. I gave her the contact information of the Grayson family. "I trust you will be sensitive to their situation. I do not want to hurt their pride."

"Don't worry, honey." She liked to call everyone honey. "I will mention that the Thanksgiving fairy came around." She laughed. "Remember that Jesus said that none of his people will go hungry."

"Thanks again, Doris."

"Don't forget us," she said.

We both said goodbye, hoping to talk again soon.

The next step was to go online and create a GoFundMe page. I was hoping to raise enough money to give the family a nice Christmas.

I was not done yet. I emailed the school staff. I let them know that there was a family in need for the holidays and that I was starting a Toys for Tots drive. I will have a bin set up in the teachers' cafeteria for any volunteer donations. I went to the back room and emptied a huge box of clothes. I found some brown paper and wrapped it around the box, and wrote Toys for Tots on all sides.

I took a breath and decided to heat up my leftovers! Yum.

I could not sleep that night, thinking about all these plans to help the Grayson family. I started thinking about how many families need help this holiday season.

The next morning Neil and Gage both came to see me during morning Cass hour. "Cass, can we talk to you?" Neil whispered.

I put my pencil down and motioned with my head to step out into the hall. "What's up, guys?"

"It's Jake, Coach," Neil started.

"He called us last night," said Gage.

I gave a forced half smile, letting them know that I knew. I was glad that Jake talked to them and brought everything out in the open. "I have started a few things that can help the family," I assured them. "There are things in the works now."

Gage talked quickly, "My mom saw your GoFundMe page last night, so we put two and two together. They already donated money last night, and both my folks called their friends. The page is blowing up."

Neil jumped right in, "How about some type of toy-drive for his younger brother and sister?'

I put my hand up. "Already set up in the faculty room."

They looked at each other. "Can we tell Jake that he doesn't have to quit the team?" Gage said.

"Yes," I replied. "Tell him things are in the works for Thanksgiving and Christmas."

"Wow, you took care of Thanksgiving too?" Gage said.

"My church will be taking care of them," I answered. I still call them my church.

Neil asked, "When the toys are collected, can we deliver them? You have made us feel like family, Cass. He is one of our family."

"I think that's a super idea," I said with a smile. "I will set that up."

All three of us put our hands on each other's shoulders and smiled.

Chapter 16

When I got to the faculty room, I could not believe all the toys that were already in my make-shift Toy for Tots box.

I saw Jake during 2nd-period gym class, and he had a big smile on his face. During the next two days of practice, Jake was like a machine, working extra hard. I am not sure how he was processing all that was going on. He did know that he had many friends and teammates who cared about him. Sometimes that is all it takes to help a person heal in life.

Just before Thanksgiving, I received a phone call from Doris Klossman. "Mickey, honey, how are you doing?"

"Doris, we have to stop meeting like this," I said. We both laughed.

"Mickey," she went on. "Our Thanksgiving committee would like to invite you to our Thanksgiving dinner next Wednesday. It is our treat. You can bring a guest," she giggled.

I thought for a minute. I was going to head up to the cabin, spend a little time there, and close it up for the winter. "That would be great, Doris." I did not say yes because I felt obligated. I said yes because I wanted to explore my feelings when I visited the church. "What time is dinner, and what can I bring."

"Dinner is at 4:00, honey." She always had that sweet tone to her voice. I knew they wanted to start dinner early so the older folks could get home and in bed by 9:00. "All you need to bring is that wonderful smile of yours."

"Bless you, Doris. Save a hug for me. See you Wednesday at 4:00" I heard her giggle as we were hanging up.

The Wednesday before Thanksgiving, I attended my former church with flowers in my hand and a plate of chocolate chip cookies. When I met Doris at the front door, I said, "These flowers are for you, dear."

"Oh my God, honey," she exclaimed. "I can't remember the last time a fine-looking gentleman brought me flowers." She got on her tiptoes and gave me a kiss on the cheek. I felt the extra makeup on my cheek, but I did not want to wipe it off.

"As we came around the corner, I was greeted by many of my parent's friends. They all wanted hugs and kept saying, "Tell Wally and Ruthie we said hi."

As I walked into the main basement hall where the dinner was to be served, I was surprised to see Jake and his family all standing up and smiling. The church had invited them for a free Thanksgiving dinner. Mr. Grayson came right over and shook my hand vigorously. "Thank you from the bottom of our hearts, Coach Cassman."

Before I could respond, Mrs. Grayson gave me a huge hug and said, "We were not sure what this year's Thanksgiving was going to be like. We are so grateful for your involvement." I saw Jake standing by the table with his two younger siblings, all smiles.

"It was my pleasure, folks. I am just so blessed to have a wonderful young man like Jake to coach. You both did a wonderful job as parents." The parents blushed, and tears were forming in their eyes. "Please enjoy your Thanksgiving meal. These folks at this church never disappoint anyone when it comes to food." We all shared a laugh. We were all assigned to the same table. The guest table.

When the meal was over, I was stuffed. I enjoyed going around to the different tables and shaking people's hands. Sharing stories from the past. Accepting condolences for the death of my fiancée. Mary and I had visited a few times, and everyone liked her. How could they not?

I pulled Mr. and Mrs. Grayson aside. "Please don't take this the wrong way," I started. We ran a Toys for Tots drive at our school, with the focus on your family." I looked at Mr. Grayson. "It got such a response that I was wondering if you know of any other people from your factory who are in the same situation. If you do, the boys on the wrestling team were going to bring the toys over to your house. However, I thought that because we have so many toys, we could probably do something at the school for all the families affected by these layoffs."

Mr. and Mrs. Grayson stood with their mouths open. Then they looked at each other. Mr. Grayson said he knew of similar families. If I set something up, he will contact the families.

"Perfect," I said. "We want all of the kids to have gifts for the holidays." I got another hug from Mrs. and a man hug from Mr. Grayson.

"One more thing," I said. I pulled out the envelope with the $4400.00 in it. It was sealed. "We did a GoFundMe page to get your family through the holidays. Please wait until you get home so as not to embarrass me. I get too emotional as it is. Just make sure you have plenty of food and supplies for the holiday and this rough winter coming up." I smiled and left before they could see the tears streaming down my cheeks.

The Toys for Tots party for the children that next Saturday ran smoothly. The school let us use the cafeteria. Ernie, my custodian buddy, helped set it up and did the cleanup. I slipped him some extra money for his service. The wrestlers were the hosts, serving cookies and juice. There were smiles around, and all the children had toys for Christmas.

Chapter 17

After an eventful November, it was time to get the season started. We had three matches before the Christmas break. The schedule was not really our friend. Our first match was against Hickory High School, which I felt confident about. The next two matches were against Wheatley and then Troy just before the Christmas break. I was hoping to have the team get more experience before wrestling those two teams. Troy was the new powerhouse in the league. We were scheduled to wrestle them in their gym.

The final varsity lineup going into the season looked quite balanced.

98 lbs.	Scott Alan
105 lbs.	Bo Bennett
112 lbs.	Leo Carter (Leo had his bright new shoes on)
119 lbs.	Jazz Cyrcle (always with his earbuds in)
126 lbs.	Tycz Brock (Tycz got his grades up thanks to his remedial teacher)

132 lbs.	Logan Tayson
138 lbs.	Gage Alan (co-Capt.)
145 lbs.	Lucas Jeter
155 lbs.	Jake Grayson
167 lbs.	William Drake
177 lbs.	Neil Ellis (co-Capt.)
Heavywt.	Nate (Bubby) Chance

Our first match against Hickory was a success. Scotty started out tough as nails. He warmed up during the National Anthem. Then he proceeded to sit on the warmup mat and remove his artificial leg. When the referee called the wrestlers into the circle, he hopped to the middle. He pinned his opponent in the second period. Bo then pinned his opponent in the first period.

We won by a team score of 49-9.

Our next match was against Wheatley, and I wish we had them later in the year. It was a close match, with big wins from Scotty, Gage, Jake, and Neil. There were some close matches that came down to the wire. The final score was Wheatley 23-Mayville 20. Poor

Bubby got pinned at the end, which wrapped up the win for Wheatley. I always told the team that it does not come down to one person.

Even though wrestling is an individual sport, there is also a team score as well. Every individual match contributes to the total team score.

Our next opponent was to be Troy. Troy had already beaten Wheatley during the first week of the season.

In a stroke of fate, as some may say. There was a huge snowstorm that canceled all the schools and, of course, our match with Troy. The schedule makers would reschedule the match with Troy sometime later in the season.

It was time for our Christmas recess. I met with the team and told them to enjoy Christmas with their families and gave them a schedule of our practices for the week between Christmas and New Year's.

"Coach Donaldson and I are very proud of how you guys have handled the preseason and the first couple of matches," I begin. "Go home and enjoy some time with your families. Enjoy Christmas. We will come back next week and go back to work. I have a few ideas on how we can improve, but for now, relax for a few days. Now, get out of here," I joked.

They all filed out yelling, "Merry Christmas, Cass."

As I was straightening up my office, Pete stayed back and stared at me. "What?" I spoke.

"What are you doing for Christmas, Mick?" Pete inquired.

"Well, I plan to relax and maybe cook for a change and make a few dinners for myself. I think I bought out the frozen food section the last time I went to the grocery store," I joked.

"Suzie and I would like to invite you over for Christmas Eve dinner." He did not seem to be finished. "Suzie has a friend....."

"Hang on there, partner," I interrupted. "Why do all JV wrestling coaches think they are my life coaches?" I was laughing. "It is a nice thought, but it smelled like a setup right from the start. Do I look like I need setting up?"

"You need something, Mick." He was smiling, but I felt his sincerity. "You are always alone. It would not hurt to meet someone you can just do things with. This girl is a nurse who works with Suzie. She is not bad on the eyes like they say! She never goes out either…."

"So, two lost souls, huh?" I was smiling. "Two ships lost at sea!" I looked at Pete. "I really appreciate it, but I'm not ready to meet someone."

"Mick, come on," he pleaded. "How can you pass up a home-cooked meal on Christmas Eve?"

"The meal sounds great, and seeing your kids would be nice." I rolled my eyes. "The setup, I am not too thrilled about. But I will come. If she gets frisky, I know my wrestling moves." We both laughed.

"Great, Mick, I will text you the address and time. Just come and relax."

"Thanks, my friend." I shook his hand.

As he was leaving and going down the gym hallway, he called Suzie. He did not know that his voice echoed when I heard him say, "I got him, Suzs. Now it's your turn to get her. And make sure she knows how to wrestle! Never mind, I will explain later."

75

"What," I yelled. "Peter, get back here." But he ran away and was gone.

Chapter 18

December 24th was always a big day growing up. Last-minute decorating the Christmas cookies, baking, and last-minute shopping.

This year I would spend Christmas Eve having dinner at my JV coach's house. I dressed in a tan pair of casual slacks. I wore a dark blue button-down shirt. I made sure my shoes shined, actually, by dusting them off. I was not trying to impress anyone, namely their other guest. It just felt good to get dressed up.

I remember going to church on Christmas Eve when we were growing up. Doris Klossman did call me and ask if I was going to attend church on Christmas Eve. I told her that I was having dinner with a friend and his family. So that was another positive for this dinner; I did not have to attend church. I always enjoyed going to church. I just must go back when I am ready.

I picked up two bottles of wine, one red and one white. I bought a game for the kids, 'Don't step in the lava.' I wrapped it up for them. I also picked up flowers for Suzie.

I was asked to be there around 3:00, so naturally, I was there at 2:45. Pete met me at the door with a big handshake. "Thanks for coming, buddy."

"Thanks for having me, Pete," I replied.

Suzie came around the corner with a big smile. "Hey, Mick. So good to see you again." I had met Suzie during some of the football get-togethers. She was a real go-getter with so much energy. She was a beautiful woman in her mid-forties. She had medium-length brown hair that moved while she walked. Suzie was very trim and fit. She liked to work out but did not have much time. She wore a beautiful pink dress.

"Thanks for having me," I reached out the flowers to her. "You look lovely tonight. These are for you."

"Aw, they are beautiful. Thank you." She smelled the bouquet. "Honey, grab his coat," she motioned to Pete.

"Here, this is a little something for the kids." I handed her the lava game. "Hopefully, they don't have this, and they will enjoy it." I could already see a couple of the girls peeking around the corner. I handed the wine to Pete. "Not sure what your preference is, but here's one of each."

"Wow, thanks, man. Let me take your coat." He hung up my coat, and I stayed by the front door. "Come on into the living room. There is someone we want you to meet."

I just smiled and stuck out my arm, indicating that he should lead the way. We walked into the living room, and standing next to Suzie was this beautiful, breathtaking blonde. Suzie held the woman's arm in both hands. "Mick, I would like to introduce you to Shell Samuels. We work together as nurses. She is an RN and taking courses to move up and…."

Pete put his hand up. Suzie was trying too hard.

The first thing I noticed about Shell was her beautiful smile. Her smile seemed to brighten up the room. She had a cute dimple on her right cheek. Shell had a beautiful purple dress and earrings to match. Her blonde hair was full length, about six inches beyond the shoulder. She wore dark boots which came up to her knees. She was about 5'3" with a trim figure. She also filled out the top of the dress nicely. I smiled and walked over to shake her hand. "It's a pleasure to meet you, Shell." I wanted to tell her how stunning she looked, but I decided to hold back. "Shell, is that a family name?" I asked.

"My mom wanted to call me Michele, and my dad wanted to call me Shelley," she said with a huge smile. "So, they compromised and named me Shell."

"Well, I think it's beautiful," I said. She nodded and smiled.

"We call her Sam most of the time," blurred out Suzie. "Sam, as in short for Samuels?"

I laughed. "That's cute."

There was a moment of silence. No one knew what to say. It was sort of awkward. Pete broke the ice. "Why don't we all sit." As we chose our seats, I could hear the daughters giggling in the background. They were enjoying this. Shell sat on the end of the couch, and I chose the chair next to the couch.

I sat rubbing my hands together, wondering if this was as awkward for Shell as it was for me. Finally, Shell and I looked at each other at the same time, and we both said, "So...." We both laughed.

"Aw how cute," Suzie said. Pete gave her a look and nodded no to her.

"You go ahead, Sam," I said. I like both of her names, Shell and Sam.

She could not stop smiling, "So, you are the wrestling coach at Mayville and work with Pete." It was more of a statement than a question.

"He's the Head Wrestling Coach," Suzie blurred out. Pete gave her a dirty look.

"Yes," I answered as I just became a man of few words. "Are you familiar with wrestling?"

"Yes. My brother used to wrestle," she stated proudly. She looked at me, waiting for my question.

"So, you are an RN and work with Suzie." I finally found the courage to speak.

"Yes. I love my job. Very rewarding." She replied.

"She's a bedside nurse," Suzie interrupted. Pete kept shaking his head.

"Very nice," I said, nodding my head and not knowing the difference. I tried to change the subject. "Pete, I've never met the rest of your family."

"Kids come in here," Pete shouted. They must have been told to wait in the other room until they were called.

The two older girls came into the room blushing, and the other three trailed behind and bumped into one another. "These are my beautiful kids; Kaeli is 12, Maris is 10, Sophia is 8, Emma is 6, and Petey is 4." Pete stood up. "Say hello to my friend Coach Cassman, kids."

"Hi, kids," I spoke. "What a beautiful family you two have."

Kaeli and Maris started giggling. "We think Scott Alan is so cute," Kaeli said. Maris was nodding. We all laughed.

"Kids, Coach Cassman brought you a gift," Suzie offered the gift to them. The kids tore into it all at once, with little Petey pushing his way to the front. He wanted to tear off his share of the paper.

"The 'floor is lava' game," they all exclaimed. "We were hoping to get this sometime because our neighbor has it, and we love playing it," Sophia said.

"Great," I replied. "Make sure you get Dad and Mom to play also."

After a few more awkward moments, Suzie said, "I think dinner is ready."

Before we ate dinner, we all joined hands in a circle, and Pete offered prayers. It was nice.

Dinner was fantastic. Suzie had made a huge ham, sweet potatoes, green beans, rolls and butter, and salad. Then when I could not eat anymore, she brought out the pies that she had made, apple and pumpkin.

Shell and I were seated next to each other. The girls could not stop looking at us and giggling. There were small conversations, but I felt nervous, and maybe Shell did as well.

There was a moment when Pete went to check on Petey in the bathroom, and Suzie asked Kaeli and Maris to help her in the kitchen.

I leaned toward Shell and whispered, "Is this awkward for you as well?"

She nodded. "Yes. I almost did not come," she whispered back.

I got a little bolder. "Would you be interested in going for a cup of coffee? Maybe we can have a conversation without 10 million eyes watching us?"

She laughed. "Yes, I would like that. Is any place open tonight?"

"How about the 'Drip and Sip, on Heron and Main? They are always open." I suggested.

"Sounds perfect," she continued to whisper. "I have been there many times because of late nights with nursing."

I looked around and stretched my neck around the corner. "We will have to leave separately. Are you up for that adventure?"

"I like it," she smiled broadly. "Are you leaving first, or am I?"

I looked up, thinking. "I will head out first and grab a table. It might be busy," I whispered jokingly. "Sounds like a plan," she said. We both did fists bumps and smiled.

Chapter 19

After dinner, even though Pete and Suzie said no, Shell and I helped them clear the table. We heard the kids playing the floor lava game and having fun. We watched them for a little bit, and we all laughed.

Then I excused myself for the evening, saying I needed to get to bed before Santa came. Little Petey had his mouth open. He probably thought that he had to do the same thing so Santa would come.

I thanked Pete and Suzie for a wonderful time and gave them both a hug. "Nice meeting you," I said to Shell as I shook her hand.

"Same to you," she replied. "Be careful driving."

"Thanks," I smiled at her. "You too."

I got to the Drip and Sip coffee house a little before 7:00. People generally seat themselves at the Drip and Sip. There were plenty of tables and booths. Just a scattering of people there. I picked a booth towards the back. I told the waitress that I would have coffee with cream and sugar. I was expecting a friend, but not sure what she was drinking. She left an empty cup.

I had a zillion thoughts going through my mind. I was not interested in meeting another woman anytime soon, if at all. I did feel comfortable with Shell. Her smile and beautiful brown eyes were very intriguing. She had a sweetness to her voice as well. Not a girly girl, sweetness. Just a genuine sweetness. I noticed that she did not wear makeup. She did not need it. She seemed very down-to-earth.

She and I were both in the same position, corralled by a friend to meet someone. So, we had that in common. She seemed as nervous and awkward as I was.

Of course, I thought of Mary. If she was looking down on me, what would she be thinking? If the tables were turned, would I want her to pursue another relationship? How long is too long after a loss to pursue a relationship? Wait! I was not even pursuing a relationship! So many thoughts.

There have always been two main reasons why I was not interested in another relationship. First, after I lost Mary, I felt guilty about how much time I spent coaching. I put so much time into my job and took away from "us time." I was not sure I could put another woman through that.

The second reason is that I felt that I had already given my heart away to Mary. She was still in my heart. I believe that you only give your heart away once in your life. So many thoughts.

Fifteen minutes later, Shell walked in looking quite stunning. I stood up and waved her over. Her beautiful smile lit up the coffee house. "Hi," she said with that sweet tone.

"Hi to you," I replied. "You made it out, yay!" We both laughed. "Let me help you with your coat." I helped her take her coat off, and she shook her head to straighten her hair. I hung up her coat on the hook near mine.

"I wasn't sure what type of coffee you like," motioning to the empty cup.

"Hazelnut, if they have it," she replied. "If not, I will take regular and look for hazelnut creamer."

The waitress came over. "Do you have hazelnut for this lovely lady?" I asked. Realizing it was not a Starbucks or a fancy barista.

"I can bring you hazelnut creamer, sweetie," she replied.

Shell looked up at her and said, "That would be great." With her beautiful smile and sweet voice attached.

"Can I call you Sam?" I asked after the waitress left. I liked both of her names.

"Absolutely," she smiled and replied. "And Mick is okay?"

"Without a doubt." We both let out a small chuckle. "So, let me break the ice here." The waitress brought her coffee, set down some hazelnut creamer, and refilled my cup. "Thank you," I said, looking up at her.

I waited for the waitress to leave. I continued. "Sam, I will go out on a limb here. I am guessing neither of us was looking forward to being set up with someone." She was looking at me and nodding. "I have been on my own for about two years since…."

"I know about your fiancée," she offered. "I am very sorry for your loss. Please continue."

"I guess the bottom line is that I was not looking to meet anyone. I thought it would be better that we get alone like this so I can explain myself."

"Mick, you don't have to explain yourself." She was very sincere. "I was not looking to meet anyone either. So at least we are a match that way." We both laughed.

I added more cream and sugar to my coffee. As I was stirring the coffee, I looked at her. "Please tell me more about Shell Samuels."

Sam and I talked for about three hours on several subjects. She offered that she was 28 years old. She went from high school directly into nursing school. She became an RN. I asked her what a bedside nurse was. She explained that a bedside nurse provides direct care to the patients and can perform more tasks. She is also taking more courses to move forward in nursing.

She dated off and on in high school, but since she started college, she has only been on a handful of dates. Sam told me that the dates she had been on never materialized into anything because none of the men had caught her interest. For most of her dates, the men had been more interested in talking about themselves. She said it is refreshing to be asked to talk about herself! Sam devotes so much time to her work that it would be hard to be in a relationship. That sounds familiar, I thought to myself. She is not looking to be in a relationship but is constantly dogged by her two older sisters, her brother, her mom, and friends like Suzie. I kept nodding in agreement. "Welcome to my world," I said.

Sam is the youngest of four children. Her mom and dad are both in education, mom teaches elementary, and dad teaches high school history. They are a very close-knit family, spending holidays and birthdays together as much as possible. Sam lives by herself but talks to her mom regularly.

When Sam is not working or studying for her class work, she likes to relax with a good book. She also enjoys yoga, which gives her calm and relaxation! She is well-rounded, watching a good sporting event, the history channel, and she even likes Hallmark movies. She is an avid football fan and is not shy when she lets the referee know that he blew a call! Sam tries to fit in a gym workout a couple of times a week. Jogging is also one of her interests. Sometimes, during a break from work, she will take a walk. It might be something as simple as walking the halls of the hospital.

When Sam was in high school, she was a pretty good athlete. Soccer, basketball, and softball were her specialties. She wishes she had more time in her schedule to attend sporting events.

She noticed my cauliflower ear on my left side. Her brother has a small one on his right ear. Cauliflower ears are predominant in the sport of wrestling. The cartilage in the ear gets dislodged from all the banging and headlocks in wrestling. It is actually a sign that wrestlers identify with.

I let Sam tell me her life story and what her interests are, then she said it was my turn. I told her about my wonderful family growing up. Going to church and enjoying the holidays. She laughed when I told her that I was named after Mickey Mantle.

I explained that in high school, I was known as a "gym rat," always hanging around the gym. I played football, wrestled, and ran track. Wrestling was my passion. I was a state champion in my senior year and excelled in college as well. So, teaching PE, coaching wrestling, and assisting in football is a dream job.

We talked about Mary, and there were tears in my eyes. She smiled when she saw my emotional side. I told her about my cabin in the mountains that I use for relaxing and getting away sometimes.

We talked about other little things. Anything and everything that came to our minds. It was refreshing for me. She was easy to talk to and a good listener. We laughed a lot. I noticed that she has different types of laughs; short laughs, long laughs, and different tones. It was cute.

We did not bother to worry about time. Eventually, we realized it was after 10:00. "Oh my God," She exclaimed. "Have we been talking for over three hours?"

I laughed. "And we drank enough coffee to stay up all night."

"Let me pay the bill, and I will walk you to your car," I offered. I got the waitress' attention and motioned with my hands that I was writing something, indicating I wanted her to bring me the bill. When she brought it over, she was smiling. "You two look so cute. First date?"

We both sort of mumbled, sort of lost for words. "We just met and are getting to know each other," I finally confessed. "What better place to do that than at the Drip and Sip." I paid the bill, gave her a nice tip and an extra $20, and said, "Merry Christmas."

I helped Sam with her coat and held the door open for her when we left. "That's my blue Ford SUV," she said as she clicked the remote, unlocking the car.

"Um…." I mumbled.

"Um?" She cocked her head and looked at me.

"I know we both have extremely busy schedules…." I paused.

"And?" She said, smiling.

"You aren't going to make this easy on me, are you?" I smiled.

"I'm just messing with you," she laughed. "I was hoping you would ask for my phone number."

We exchanged cell numbers. I held the car door open for her. We both wished each other a Merry Christmas as she drove away.

I think I was going to try to schedule a session with Dr. Helen Morgan, my therapist.

Chapter 20

Thank you for getting together this evening. Please text me when you get home safe and sound. Mick.

That was my text to Sam when I got home. I planned on going up to the cabin for Christmas Day and coming back the next day. Practice will resume on the 27th. I packed my supplies and got my cooler prepared to load in the morning. Before long, I heard a ding on my phone. I had a text message.

Made it home safe and sound. (a smile emoji) Thank you again for getting together and for the coffee. Thx also for our talk and for being open. It felt good to share my thoughts with you. Hopefully, you felt the same. Hey, we survived the "setting up" together! (Laughy face) Sam

Yay! Glad you are home safe and sound. Yes, I feel the same as you. It was refreshing to open up to you. Thx. (Smiley face) Enjoy Christmas Day. You mentioned that you would be with family, enjoy. (Smiley face) I will be heading up to the cabin and spending Christmas there. Mick

Please be very careful driving tomorrow (snow emoji) and enjoy the outdoors. (Smiley face)

She was beginning to text something else, then stopped. She must have been thinking about what she wanted to say. She started up again.

It would be alright to text me to let me know that you are okay with your trip to the mountains (smiley face)

That's a deal. Nighty night! I wanted to send a hug emoji. I just sent another smiley face. She sent back a huge smiley face.

I woke up Christmas morning thinking about Sam. My friends and family were probably correct. It is nice to have someone to share moments with. I could not help but send her a morning text.

Good morning and Merry Christmas to my new friend! (Christmas tree) Enjoy the day with your family. (Smiley face)

Sam woke up Christmas morning feeling good about meeting Mickey the previous evening. Sam has been so involved with her work and schooling that she really had not thought about dating. When she gets home from work, she likes to relax, maybe take a bubble bath. She liked being alone and never thought about loneliness or being with a partner. Sam smiled when she thought how much fun it was with Mickey at the coffee shop.

Were her feelings about being with someone changing? She was struggling with that thought, but it was way too early to think about a relationship. Mickey was a gentleman, and he seemed generally interested in her and her feelings. That was very nice. Sam felt comfortable with Mickey, and it was nice to share thoughts with a male friend. Sam decided that she would like to see Mickey again and see where that friendship would lead. She was anxious to return a text message. She checked out the weather in the mountains for Mickey.

Merry Christmas to you as well, Mick. (Santa emoji) I have already checked the weather for you, and it seems like it is going to be a nice day in the mountains. (Sun emoji) I told her last night about my cabin and where it was located. She already checked the weather for me! That made me smile!

Wow, thx. You should actually be sleeping because of your big day today.

Couldn't sleep....too much caffeine!!!!!

Same!

Be safe out there, Mick!

Thx, you as well, Sam! And thx again for last evening!

After much thought, I decided to send a "hug" emoji. She dinged a "hug" emoji right back.

I was going to call my parents and wish them a Merry Christmas, but I figured they were in church. I will call them later. I called my brother and sister-in-law in New England and wished them a Merry Christmas.

Martha said, "Another Christmas alone, Mick?" Should I mention I had coffee for three hours last night with someone I just got introduced to? I decided to wait on that subject.

"I am heading up to the cabin soon. Alone is not a bad thing when I have the beauty of nature all around me," I replied.

She was not buying it. "Nice try, kiddo. You need to find a pretty little thing to share those times with." Now, I was glad I did not tell her yet. There would have been too many questions and not enough answers.

"Listen, you guys enjoy your day," I changed the subject. "And don't drink too much eggnog" We wished each other well and hung up.

I sent a text to Dr. Morgan.

Merry Christmas, Dr. Morgan. I assume you will not read this until tomorrow, but I would like to schedule a session as soon as possible. I met someone. I would like to discuss this with you. Thx, Mickey Cassman. A text to a therapist must be short, not elaborate. I was surprised when she answered immediately.

Merry Christmas to you, Mick. Let us figure out a time. I will text you my openings. Her response was very business-like. She did not say, "That is great news," or anything like that. She was professional and will save her remarks for our private sessions.

We scheduled an appointment for 2:00 on the 28th. I have practice in the morning. I am looking forward to our session. Sam is in my thoughts, and I need to talk things out with Dr. Helen Morgan.

Chapter 21

The weather at the cabin was perfect for this time of year. Sam was correct with her weather report. The ground was covered in a beautiful blanket of snow. The sun was shining and glistening on the snow.

After unpacking, I made a pot of coffee. As the coffee was brewing, I built a fire in the fireplace. I poured myself a cup and stirred in my cream and sugar. I moved a dining room chair near the back window, overlooking the lake. I sat with my coffee and looked out at the beauty. If I had any artistic ability, this would be a great picture to paint. That was not going to happen.

I like to come to this place to think, reflect, and plan. I had much to think about. I wondered about my feelings for Sam. Was she thinking about me, as well?

The practice was scheduled for the 27th. I needed to let the team know how far they had come from the beginning of the year. Even though the team record was just 1-1, I wanted to give them a purpose for the remainder of the year. I had confidence in them. I needed them to instill confidence in themselves.

I put on my snow boots and took a nice walk down by the lake. I walked around the lake. Sometimes I would run into one of my neighbors. Not today. It was Christmas day. They were all with family.

After lunch, I called my mom on her cell phone. "Mickey, dear," she answered. There was music and lots of yelling in the background. "Merry Christmas, dear."

"Merry Christmas, Mom," I replied. "What's all that noise?"

"We are at a driveway party on our street, with a band and dancing." They live in a retirement community, which is like Disney Land for adults.

"I'm happy you guys are enjoying yourselves," I shouted. "How's dad."

"He is doing great, Mickey. He is out in the street doing the electric slide." She laughed.

"Listen, Mom, I will not hold you up. Go out and show them how you can shake!" I was laughing with her. "I just wanted to tell you I love you guys and Merry Christmas. By the way, Doris Klossman from church sent her helloes, and they miss you at church."

"We both love you too, dear." She had to shout over the noise. "It is great to hear Doris' name and give a hello from us. Tell me, are you alone at the cabin again this year." I knew that was coming.

"I'm okay, Mom. I'm enjoying nature. Go enjoy yourself."

Mom sighed loudly. "You know I worry about you, dear." It sounds like she got off her chair and moved to a quieter place. "We both worry about you being alone." This is not the first or even the second time she has said that.

"Mom, I'm good," I tried to assure her. "I love you!"

"We send our love too, dear. Bye."

It was a quiet day at the cabin. Just what I needed. I kept myself busy splitting wood and doing some odd jobs around the cabin. I went into my office in the spare room and worked on my notes for the coming days of practice.

I cooked myself a casserole of pasta primavera. It would give me plenty of leftovers for the upcoming week. Mom would always make a big ham dinner for Christmas when we were growing up. Those are great memories.

I was able to get enough reception on the TV to watch a football game. I grabbed a beer and watched the game by the fire.

Around 8:00, my phone dinged. I looked at the screen. It was a text from Sam.

Hey, Mick, how was your day at the cabin? I smiled when I got the text. I was wondering how long she thought about sending me a text before she actually sent one. I wanted to respond immediately.

Hey backatcha, Sam. The day at the cabin was beautiful. You were spot on with the weather report. I had a nice relaxing day. Me and nature. How was the day with your family?

It was nice. It always is. But OMG, I mentioned that you and I went for coffee for 3 hours last night, and all chaos broke out! I should have kept that detail to myself!!!! I'm jealous of your day in nature!

Aw, I'm sorry you went through that. You will have to share those stories with me sometime. My mom and sister-in-law each brought the topic up, but I changed the subject.

I should have done the same thing. What's done is done. I just wanted to let you know I was thinking about you....is that okay to say???? (Fingers crossed emoji)

It's absolutely okay to say. In fact, I must admit that you were on my mind today as well! (Smiley face)

Great. Sleep well tonight, and stay away from that caffeine tonight! (Two laughy faces)

Ha-ha. You sleep well yourself, Sam. Hugs to you! (Hug emoji)

Hugs backatcha! (Two hug emojis)

My Christmas day just got much better!

Chapter 22

When I got up the next morning, I made coffee and sent Sam a text.

Good morning, Sam. I know you are scheduled to work today. Just wanted to wish you a safe drive to work.

I'm here already. I got called in early. I appreciate the text! You are such a caring person! Gotta run. Let's chat later.

You bet. Go save lives! Hugs! (Hug emoji)

Thx again. Your morning text made me smile. Hugs! (Smiley face and two hug emojis) I thought how nice it would be to finally hug Sam. All we did was shake hands. I guess a person can be more daring in a text message.

The day was the same as yesterday. For the first time in a long time, I *did* feel lonely. Sam would enjoy the cabin getaway. I would enjoy having her.

I packed up earlier than normal and headed back to my home. I had the 2:00 appointment on the 28th with Dr. Morgan etched in mind.

When I got home to Syracuse Lane, I did some odd jobs around the house. I changed a light bulb and replaced a leaky gasket in the toilet flusher, among other things. It was interesting that as time went on after losing Mary, I always felt comfortable in my home. I never felt like I was lonely or needed someone there with me.

After meeting and texting with Sam, I started to feel different. I kept wondering what she was doing during the day. What was she thinking about? Ding.

Hi! I'm on a break. Just wanted to say hi (Wave emoji). I smiled!

Hi yourself! Is it okay to say I was just thinking about you? You just put a smile on my face! (Smile emoji)

You have a beautiful smile! (Smile emoji)

Thx! Yours lights up the whole room! (Smile emoji)

Gotta run! Hugs! (Hug emoji)

Hugs! (Hug emoji)

It was very cool that she would text me on her break or lunch. I think we are both smitten! I texted her later in the evening because another storm was coming through. I asked her to text me when she got home safe and sound.

She texted me when she got home. Then I called her, and we talked for about two hours. We shared with each other how our day went. I laughed when she told me the stories from her family get-together on Christmas when she told them about me. She said it was not funny, and then she burst out laughing. Her laughing made me laugh even more.

We wished each other a good night's sleep. She had work early tomorrow, and I had practice in the morning and errands to run in the afternoon. We both said "hugs" to each other. I wondered if she was as anxious as I was to be in each other's arms!

Chapter 23

December 27th was a big day for our team. I was excited to get back into the practice room and get them focused for the second half of the season. I also have a hop in my step because of Sam. I sent her a morning text over coffee, then headed to school. She sent me back a nice text.

It was good to see all the kids. They would stop by my office and show me things that they got for Christmas. A few got new wrestling shoes. There were brand-name tee shirts, new winter coats, etc. Gage and Scotty came into the locker room debating a referee's call from a college football bowl game the previous day. Those two were always watching and talking about sports. Jake peaked into the office and said his parents were thrilled with the money. His dad made sure some of his co-workers got the food that they needed. He was also getting called back to work soon.

When everyone was up in the wrestling room, I started with a meeting.

"Gentlemen," I started and looked around the wrestling room. Some boys were sitting up against the wall. Others were kneeling, while others were lying on their side with their head propped up by their arm. I looked at Jazz. "Jazz," I said as I made a motion to take his earbuds out. Everyone laughed.

"First of all, welcome back," I continued. "I trust you all had a wonderful Christmas with your family and friends. Hopefully, you are all rested. I must admit, I have been around wrestling for a long time, and the accomplishments you have made already this year are amazing. You have literally turned this program around from a last-place team to a contending team." The boys looked at one another. "Sure, we lost to Wheatley, but I am not done coaching you yet. I plan to push you guys harder over the next four days. We are still in the running for the championship." The boys shared different quizzical looks. They had never been told that before. "I am going to give you my best. If you guys…." I paused and looked them in the eyes. "If you guys give me everything you have in practice, we can reach any goal that we set." There was silence. The boys who were lying down sat up.

"Guys, I am ready to start a dream. A dream of finishing this season in first place as champions. I put my fist up in the air and yelled "Starting a dream." One by one, they got up and joined me in the center of the mat, yelling, "Starting a dream." Their fists joined mine, and we chanted together. "Starting a dream, starting a dream!"

The remainder of the practice was intense. I demonstrated some of the moves and their finishes. Some of the boys were not finishing their moves in earlier matches. We drilled over and over what I taught. The boys knew that I was big on repetition. The more times you practice a move, the likelihood it will work in a match.

After the drilling sessions, there was a full go with sparing partners. There was so much intensity that the sweat was pouring off their bodies. Toward the end of practice, the boys would grab a partner, and I would time them in a practice match. High school wrestling matches are six minutes in length, 3 two-minute periods. Our practice matches were nine minutes in length, 3 three-minute periods. It was intended to get them in condition. If they could finish a grueling nine-minute match in practice, they would be in shape to wrestle a six-minute match in a meet.

I was always big on cardiovascular training. Some people call it "wind conditioning." I wanted my wrestlers to be the best-conditioned team on the mats. After practice, we went to the gym. I had the wrestlers change out of their wrestling shoes and into regular sneakers. We would run wind sprints up and down the gym floor.

Some coaches will have their wrestlers run for a mile for wind conditioning. Wrestling is not a long-distance sport but rather a sport of short bursts. I am of the theory that short, quick sprints are better for wrestlers' endurance.

After practice, some of the kids wanted me to open the weight room and lift weights. I told them that with the intensity of the first day back, they should go home and rest their bodies. They will be sore in the morning. The soreness will go away after a few days when their bodies get used to the intensity.

Later that evening, Sam and I talked for about an hour and a half. We would laugh at something, then laugh at the other person laughing. I was enjoying life with her. I could not wait to talk things out with Dr. Morgan tomorrow afternoon.

Chapter 24

December 28th was very similar to the previous day. Over coffee, Sam and I texted back and forth. She was already at work but found time to sneak in a few text messages. Along with a few hug emojis!

When the boys got to practice, they admitted to being sore. No one complained. We were focused on our dream! The motivation was again in the room. More moves were taught and drilled over and over. The nine-minute matches were very intense.

The sprinting in the gym was very competitive. Even Scotty, with his artificial leg off, was hopping his sprints. The team kept cheering him on. I stood and smiled and nodded at the comradery this team was forming. Bubby was usually the last in his group to finish, but the rest of the guys kept cheering him on. The spirit was building!

I decided to hang up some sayings referring to reaching your dreams. These were two of the signs posted. The wrestlers probably did not recognize either of these great individuals. I had to explain who they were in our history. The messages on the signs were the important part:

"A dream doesn't become a reality through magic; it takes sweat, determination, and hard work."

Colin Powell

"We all have dreams. But in order to make dreams come into reality, it takes an awful lot of determination, dedication, self-discipline, and effort."

Jesse Owens

I arrived at 1:45 for my 2:00 appointment with Dr. Helen Morgan. I was both anxious and nervous. I tried reading some of the magazines in the waiting room. My mind kept drifting. So many thoughts of Mary, Sam, and life. I was hoping Dr. Morgan would help me make sense of it all.

Dr. Morgan was punctual. At exactly 2:00, she opened her door and invited me into her office. I sat on the 2-person couch while she sat across from me on her chair, with a pad and pen in her lap. I noticed boxes of Kleenex tissues in various spots around the room.

We started out with pleasantries. She and her husband took a few days before Christmas and went on a cruise. I told her about the wrestling team. I talked about my time alone and at the cabin. Then the conversation turned to Sam. I told her how we met. She listened as I explained how we text and talk every day. I told her how much fun we had together and how good I felt when we just talked.

"I need to make sense of it all, Dr. Morgan," I said. "There were always two main reasons why I was leery of another relationship. One is because the time I put into my coaching takes away from time with a partner. After I lost Mary, I regretted the time that I did not spend with her. I was not sure I wanted to put another woman through that routine." Dr. Morgan heard me say this before. She just sat and nodded.

"The second reason," I continued. "In no particular order was the heart thing." She knew what I was talking about. She smiled and said, "Go on."

"I gave my heart away to Mary," I said. "You can only give your heart away once?" It was a question more than a statement. "Mary is still in my heart. She will always be there. I am confused with the feelings that I have for Sam."

Dr. Morgan smiled. "Mick, the first dilemma that you are having is easy. You and Sam both have very busy and demanding schedules.

You mentioned that she admitted it was part of her concern with relationships. You found someone whose work and schooling take up much of her time. She does not have or at least takes enough time to give to a partner. Sound familiar?" She smiled.

"Yes, it sure does," I nodded.

"When you and Sam get together," she continued. "You two are lucky and have an advantage that other couples don't have." I gave her a quizzical look. "You kids will have quality time together. Some couples who are together 24/7 do not appreciate each other as much as you and Sam can. When you get together, it will be quality time." That all made sense.

"Now, let me talk about the heart issue," Dr. Morgan continued. "You never gave your heart away, Mick. You have a wonderful heart. Just look at how you have touched the students and wrestlers that you coached over the past few years. You have given the boys and their families new meaning in life. You have lifted spirits and brought smiles to many faces. A person without a heart could not accomplish what you have accomplished."

"What you did when you met Mary was to open your heart to love for a woman. I refer to the heart as having many doors, not in the literal anatomy sense, but in the imagining sense. Imagine a door opening, and you allow Mary to enter your heart. The door stays open, and the love and passion are overflowing! When you lost Mary, that door closed! The love and passion for a woman, or wanting a woman as a partner, closed inside that door. Now the vibes that you are getting with Sam are knocking on that door. It is your choice if you want to open that door to Sam and let her in."

She noticed me tearing up. She motioned to the Kleenex box. She knows how emotional I can get. I even tear up at movies. I take a Kleenex and wipe my eyes.

"I know Mary is still in your heart," she continued. "It is okay to allow another woman into that door. I mentioned that the heart has many doors. Let us talk about children, for example. When parents have their first child, a different door opens in their hearts. They bring that child through that door and give that baby all the love and compassion that is inside that door of their hearts. When a second child is born, they bring that baby through the same door and give them the same love and compassion as the first child. Parents have so much space in that room for all their children."

"Mick, I can tell by your interactions with Sam that you are allowing the door of love to open slightly. You are afraid that if you open that door wide, there will not be room for both women in that part of your heart. I am suggesting that if you open that door wide for Sam, your love and passion will again be overflowing. Inside that door is so much love and passion for a woman. You physically lost Mary, but her memories will always remain inside that door of your heart. There is definitely room for Sam if you wish."

The tears were streaming down my cheeks. Dr. Morgan was smiling. She made so much sense. The next thing she said really brought me to tears.

"One more point. You had mentioned if the tables were turned. If you had, unfortunately, lost your life. You would want Mary to find someone and be happy. I truly believe that Mary will help you to open that door and welcome Sam into that room in your heart. She knows that Sam will make you happy!"

I always felt embarrassed showing my emotional side. People say it is a good thing.

I thanked Dr. Morgan profusely. She cleared up so many of my thoughts. So many of my trepidations. She smiled and offered me good luck. "I do not think you will need luck, Mick. Your wonderful heart will tell you what to do. Call me anytime if you need a follow-up visit." We shook hands. I wanted to hug her, but that would not have been appropriate.

I smiled, and I felt on top of the world on the ride home. A few days ago, I had many questions and not enough answers. Today, I felt I had so many answers.

Chapter 25

When I got home, I texted Sam.

Please call me tonight so we can talk. She knew I had an appointment with Dr. Morgan. I wanted to assure her that it was a good conversation. I sent another text.

It was a wonderful session. She cleared up many things in my mind. I'm looking forward to talking to you. I can't wait to see you, Sam! (Smiley face and hug emoji)

She cannot always respond immediately because of work. About 30 minutes later, my phone dinged.

I'm glad it went well. Can't wait to chat tonight. You just put a huge smile on my face! My co-workers think I won the lottery or something! (Laughy emoji) Hugs to you, Mick! (Two hug emojis)

Sam was anxious all day at work. She hurried home and called me as she was walking in the door. "Hey Coach, I am home. Just taking off my coat and setting my purse down."

"Wait," I said. "You must be hungry. Why don't you grab a bite to eat and call…."

"No way, mister," she interrupted me. "Tell me everything!"

I laughed. "You are hilarious," I said. She gave one of her many laughs.

First, I told her what Dr. Morgan said about our two busy schedules. She said that when we get together, we will be lucky because our time will be quality time. "That makes sense," she said.

I told Sam about Dr. Morgan's theory about the doors of the heart. I told her everything she said about opening the door to my love for a woman in my heart and how Mary would help me open that door. I heard Sam sniffling on the other end of the phone. I assumed it was good sniffling.

"Sam," I said. "I like you very much and…."

"I like you very much too, Mick," she blurted out through sniffling. "Oops, sorry for interrupting."

I laughed. "Sam, I want you to be my girlfriend." I thought about this on the way home. I decided to be direct. "I want to see you as much as we possibly can. You make me feel good when we are together. You make me laugh. You bring joy into my heart. I want to hold you and give you physical hugs, not just our emoji hugs. Let's give it a try and see where it takes us."

I finished, and there was silence on the other end for a long time. When she talked, I could tell she was crying. "Oh Mick, I don't care what time it is. Please come over and hold me. We can just sit on the couch and hold each other."

"I'm on my way," I said.

"Just be careful driving so you get here safe," she said. We both said hugs, and I was out the door.

When I got to Sam's house, I walked up to the door and was ready to knock. She opened the door and flew into my arms. We hugged on the doorstep for a long time. We both needed that warmth and comfort.

We went to the couch holding hands. We did not say a word. We sat down together, and she came into my arms again, with her head against my chest. I held her tight. We squeezed each other tight and would not let go.

After a while, I said, "I guess we are officially a 'thing'"

She raised her head and looked at me. "We are a wonderful 'thing'" Then she went back to my chest.

We hugged. We rubbed the other person's back as we hugged. We rubbed the back of the other person's head as we hugged. Dr. Morgan was correct. This was a wonderful quality time.

After about 15 minutes, I said, "Aren't you hungry?"

"No," she replied. "Are you?"

"I'm good. I have what I need right here," I said.

"Me too," she said.

We laid back on the couch in each other's arms. Eventually, we fell asleep.

We woke up at the same time, about 12:30. I looked down at her. "Hey, girlfriend."

She smiled up at me, eyes half open. "Hey, boyfriend," she said in a half-asleep tone.

"I have to go, and you have to get your butt to bed," I said. "We both have early days tomorrow."

"Aw, you have to go?" She was still half asleep.

"Yes," I replied. "We both know that I can't stay."

"I know," she said with a pouting face.

"Why don't you go get ready for bed," I said. "Then I will come in and tuck you in."

"Okay, but only if you text me when you are home safe and sound!" She had a concerned look on her face.

"Deal." We gave each other fist bumps.

Sam went into the bedroom. We both knew it was not time for a sleepover. We wanted to do things right with this relationship. After a while, she called me in. "I'm ready!"

I entered her bedroom, and she looked so cute, snuggled under the covers. I went over and made sure they were tucked under her chin. "Are you warm enough?" I was rubbing her head.

"Yes, nice, comfy, and cozy. Don't forget to text me when you get home."

"Yes, ma'am," I smiled. I reached down and rubbed her head. "Good night, Sam."

She grabbed my forearm with her hand as I was about to leave. "Can I say something to Suzie tomorrow?"

"You had better," I replied. "Because I'm going to tell Pete, and women certainly want to be the first to know!" We both laughed.

"Bye," she said in her sweet voice.

When I got home, I texted Sam that I was home safe and sound. I thanked her for letting me come over and see her. I told her that I had missed her already.

She texted back that she stayed awake until I got home safe and sound! She was missing me, as well.

I prayed and thanked Mary for helping to open the door to that room of my heart.

Chapter 26

December 29th and 30th were practically the same routine. I texted Sam over coffee before heading to practice. The first day she texted that when she told Suzie, Suzie let out a blood-curdling scream. All the nurses were wondering what was wrong. Sam thought it was hilarious.

Suzie asked Sam, "Did you sleep with him yet?

"No," she replied. "It's not like that. We are trying to do things right. Sort of taking it slow."

Suzie said in a high-pitched tone, "That's old fashion, girlfriend!" There was more. She will fill me in later. All the nurses are telling her that she is walking around the floor with the biggest smile they have ever seen on her! She is soaking it all up. Sam has a great sense of humor.

When I got to school, I told Pete. Pete shook my hand and put his other hand on my shoulder. "That's great news, buddy. Hope you will invite me to the wedding!"

"Don't get ahead of yourself, Coach." I nodded my head. "We are taking it slow."

"Come on, man," he exclaimed. "You aren't a spring chicken anymore."

I laughed. "So that makes you what? An old hen?" All guy humor.

The practice was again intense. I could see, during practice on the 30th, how the boys were improving. They were finishing their moves better. Their muscles were getting toner. They were faster on their feet. Their cardio was getting stronger. This team was turning into a well-oiled machine.

Towards the end of practice on the 30th, I gave them the option of taking the next two days off. They voted unanimously to come to practice on the morning of the 31st.

This team was 'Starting a dream!'

Sam's schedule was very busy on the 29th and 30th. We did our best to communicate, but it was not easy. One of the things she worked on was trying to find time when we could go out to dinner and celebrate being boyfriend and girlfriend. She was working 12 hours straight for three days in a row. Her schedule had her off on the 31st and New Year's Day.

We decided that we would "dress to the nines" and go out to dinner on December 31st. We were looking for someplace where she could have fresh seafood, and I would have a huge bone-in rib eye. I let her pick the restaurant. She made a reservation for 4:00, figuring we could get out of the restaurant before all the crazies got there for New Year's Eve.

The restaurant was about 45 minutes in bad weather from her house. I told her I would pick her up at 3:00, so we could get to the restaurant at 3:45.

The weather forecast was not favorable. The snow and wind were picking up. A storm was brewing. I arrived at her house around 2:45. That was on time for me. My motto is; early is on time, on time is late, and late is unacceptable. I brought her a bouquet of roses. Sam was so impressed she almost started to cry. "They are beautiful."

Because of the weather, we decided not to get too dressy. Instead of a dress, she wore gray slacks that widened at the bottom. She wore a light tan top with a black vest over the top. Her earrings and necklace were silver. Her hair was up in a bun. She wore one of her favorite pairs of boots. My mouth was open when I saw her, "you are gorgeous, Sam. You are very stunning."

"Thank you, and look how dapper you are." She ran her hand over my sleeve. I wore dark gray slacks, a blue sport coat, and a light blue button-down shirt. The collar was open. "Come on in. Let me put these in water and get my coat."

As we were leaving her house, the wind was really whipping up. She held my arm tight. I opened her door for her and had to hold it tight in the wind. When I got in the car, we looked at each other. "Are we nuts?" We both said it at the same time and laughed. She shrugged. "I'm game if you are."

I smiled. "I have been looking forward to this evening. Let's give it a try." I put the jeep in drive and started slowly.

We were about 20 minutes from the restaurant when her phone dinged. "Oh, my God!" She had a confused look on her face.

"What's wrong?" I said. I did not want to look at her because of the road conditions.

"The restaurant just closed because of the weather! They messaged anyone who had a reservation." She looked at me with droopy eyes. She turned on the Jeep radio and tuned into a local news station.

The radio announcer was warning everyone about the high winds and the blizzard conditions. They were asking everyone to stay home. Everything was closing! I put my turn signal on to make a left turn. "I have an idea. We are close to my place. I suggest we go to my house. What do you think, Sam?"

"Sure, that makes sense." She sounded worried.

"I'm not going to let anything happen to you," I assured her. She rubbed my arm. "Okay, I trust you."

I drove very slowly. The visibility was getting worse. When we turned onto Syracuse Lane, the street was almost one large snow bank. Luckily, my jeep with the 4-wheel drive was able to maneuver around the piles of snow. As I pulled into my driveway, I opened my garage with the remote.

I pulled into the garage and hit the remote to close the garage door. I looked at Sam. She had been nervous but now seemed relieved. I put my arm around her and gave her a hug. "We are safe. Let's go in and warm up."

My garage is attached to the house, so we were safe from the storm. We walked into the house. Sam turned to me and hugged me. "I was so scared," she said. "Thank you for getting us home safely."

"You're welcome," I replied as I breathed a sigh of relief. "Rain check on the dinner?"

She replied, "I'm going to hold you to that, Mister." She let out one of her short laughs.

Chapter 27

I hung up our wet coats in the laundry room. "Make yourself at home while I make a fire in the fireplace. Then I will throw something together for us to eat."

"Let me help, Mick."

As I made the fire, Sam rummaged through the refrigerator, looking for something to eat. "I have these gourmet dinners," I yelled over to her. "Leftover Monday, leftover Tuesday, you get the menu." I heard her laugh behind the refrigerator door.

I walked behind her and gave her a hug. "Find anything interesting?"

"This pasta primavera looks good. Throw it in the microwave, and voila!" And that is what we did. Pasta primavera leftovers and a glass of white wine for our celebration dinner.

After dinner, we took a second glass of wine and sat on the floor near the fireplace. We put a pillow between us to rest our arms on. "This was a nice idea coming here, Mick," she seemed relieved.

"I have another idea." She looked at me. "I think you should sleep here tonight." She brought her head back in surprise. "What I'm saying is you can sleep in the guest bed. It's very comfortable."

She looked up like she was thinking. "I didn't bring any change of clothes. Anything to sleep in."

"I will give you a tee shirt, a pair of gym shorts, and some wool socks," I suggested. "I also have extra toothbrushes. Unused, of course!"

We laughed. Then she looked me in the eyes. She nodded slowly and pursed her lips. "I think you are correct. Bring on the pj's. What a fashion statement this will be." She said the last part while laughing.

When she came out of the bedroom with my New York Yankee tee shirt and blue gym shorts on, she looked amazing. The no-bra look with the tee shirt was a killer. She turned around with her arms out like she was posing in a fashion show. "I will give you a 10 for fashion, my dear," I remarked.

She looked up like she was still posing. "Really? I think I am more of a 10 plus."

We both laughed hard. "Come here, you nut," I motioned her to sit next to me on the couch.

"Now what?" She asked.

Well, since this is supposed to be a romantic night," I begin. "Let's watch a romantic Hallmark movie. Then, if we are still awake, we can watch the ball drop in Times Square." I knew that Sam had worked long hours and might not make midnight.

So, our celebration night for becoming boyfriend and girlfriend consisted of leftover pasta and watching a Hallmark movie. But we did not care. We were together. We snuggled on the couch and enjoyed the movie.

When the movie was over, she said, "Aw, that was sweet." She looked at me, and I had tears in my eyes. "Aw, you teared up. That is sweet."

"I actually get embarrassed when I do that," I offered. "I can't help it. It's a crazy emotional thing."

"I don't think it's crazy," she said in her sweet voice. "I think it's adorable. And you are adorable," as she hugged me.

We snuggled on the couch for a while, and then I could feel her dozing off. "Hey, why don't I put you to bed." I smiled at her.

"But I want to see the ball drop." She was barely awake.

"Come on, let me tuck you in." I got Sam to her feet slowly. "We can watch it on YouTube in the morning. You need your sleep." She was almost asleep when her head hit the pillow. I rubbed her forehead and brushed my hand over her hair. "Good night, sweet dreams."

"Good night," She was out immediately.

I went by the fireplace and barely stayed awake myself. I watched the ball drop in Times Square. It just became a new year. What would that new year have in store for Sam and me? I *think* I have some answers now.

What would the new year bring for the Mayville wrestling team? I *hope* I have the answers to that.

I went to bed by myself. I tossed and turned. I tried to count sheep, but that never works. I kept thinking about the woman I cared about sleeping in the other room. Finally, I got up and walked over to her bedroom door. I opened it slowly. Sam was sleeping on her left side, facing the window. I stood over the bed for a moment. I opened the covers and slid into the bed. I put my arm around her waist and cuddled up behind her. We fit perfectly together.

"Hey, coach," she mumbled in a groggy tone. "Thanks for joining me."

"You are tough to resist." I hugged her. Then I moved my arm up around her chest, laying my hand over her breasts. "Is this okay?"

There was silence as I waited for her answer. She rubbed my forearm with her hand. "You have soft skin. Sleep tight." That meant that she was okay with the position of my hand. That was as far as my intentions were. We slept very soundly.

Chapter 28

I woke up early. I was still holding onto the beautiful Shell Samuels. It felt great waking up next to her. I slipped out of bed and let her sleep.

I made coffee. I had bought hazelnut in case she was ever over for coffee. Perfect timing! I brewed hers, as well as regular for me.

As I sat with my first cup of coffee, I was thinking. This was a new year. This was a new year for Sam and me. How fitting it was that we met this time of year and we are starting a new year together. Just like my wrestling team, Sam and I could also be STARTING A DREAM!

Another hour passed, then I heard rustling in her room. She came out with her hair disheveled, but she still looked great! I got up and started to say good morning when she quickly rushed into my arms. She hugged me with her head on my chest and kept saying, "Thank you, thank you!"

"What's going on, kiddo?" I said as I hugged her.

She continued. "Thank you for being a gentleman and respectful and a sweetheart. Most guys would have taken advantage of me last night. You did not. You are different, a good different. I feel safe with you, Mickey Cassman." She held me tight.

After a pause, I pulled her away so I could look into her beautiful brown eyes. "You're welcome. Now, you owe me something." She cocked her head and gave a quizzical look. "Happy New Year, Sam. You know what couples do on New Year's Eve?"

She looked into my eyes. "Yes, I do. I think it's time to collect."

Slowly, I turned my head. I lowered my lips towards hers. We closed our eyes together as our lips went into an amazing kiss. Not overly passionate. Not a peck on the lips. Just a nice soft joining of the lips. When I picked my head up, I smiled. "That was beautiful," I said. "Just as I dreamed it would be." She got up on her tiptoes, and we kissed again and held each other tight.

It was New Year's Day. We had the entire day to ourselves to do what we wanted. We sat by the fire with our coffee. "Wait a minute," she exclaimed. "This is hazelnut! Did you get this for me?" I nodded and got another kiss. This was fun!

We sat and kissed, and snuggled, and kissed, and chatted, and kissed some more. It felt good to kiss. I told her about the wrestling team and how this past week, we started a dream. "Now, I want to start a dream with you, Shell Samuels!"

"I'm all in!" She leaned in and gave me a big kiss. "You and I are starting a dream. Sealed with a kiss!" Then we kissed to seal our 'starting a dream' together!

The storm had stopped, and the sun was out. What a crazy weather pattern. The plows were going to be working on getting everyone out of their homes. We did not care. We were in our own little world. We could do anything, anytime we wanted.

I made us a nice breakfast of sausage and eggs. I knew she preferred turkey sausage, so I had some in the freezer. I served breakfast with English muffins and orange juice.

We were like two teenagers, goofy and giddy! While I was cooking the eggs, she came up behind me. She hugged me and started kissing my neck; it gave me chills. "Hey, are you trying to bribe the cook to get more eggs?" She said, "No, you just looked so kissable!" We laughed. I told her about my dad. He liked to cook on the grill when we were growing up. My dad is a funny guy. He had a barbeque apron that read 'Kiss the cook.' Sam said she would get me one for my birthday.

When she was washing dishes after breakfast, I came up behind her and started kissing *her* neck. "Oh," she laughed and squirmed. "That tickles and you are bothering the help," I told her she looked so kissable. She turned around and threw her arms around my neck, and gave me a big kiss. Soapy water went all over me and the floor, so we laughed.

We bundled up and went outside. She wore what she had on last evening, plus the warmer stuff that I gave her. She looked so cute in an oversized beanie and oversized gloves. "I look frumpy," she laughed. "You look like a cute frumpy," I replied as I kissed what little face she had showing inside her scarf.

We ran around the backyard, yelling in the air. We yelled silly things that made no sense, like little kids. We walked hand in hand, high-stepping through the drifts. We hugged as we looked at the beauty of the sun glistening on the snow covering the area. We talked about the beauty of nature. I told her about the cabin and the beauty of the lake, and nature around the lake. In our busy lives, we sometimes do not take the time to appreciate this beauty. We decided that we would take trips to the cabin as often as we could to be with nature.

We built a snowman. We named him 'snowy.' We talked to Snowy. "Hey, snowy, happy New Year," I said. We both just realized that in past years, we would be alone, and we would be calling our parents to wish them a happy New Year. We looked at each other and shrugged and laughed.

Sam looked at Snowy. "Hey, snowy, this is my boyfriend, and we slept together last night!" We could not stop laughing at that one. After a while, she put her arms around my neck and leaned against me, and said to Snowy, "And we *started a dream* today!" We kissed.

I turned my back and faced the house when a snowball hit me in the back! "Hey!" I shouted. "Don't start something you can't finish, sister!" She was already running away.

"Catch me if you can!" She yelled with her head in the air. I high-stepped through the snow. When I caught her, I tackled her, and we rolled. She looked up with snow all over her face. "Ugh," she laughed with a snowy face. I brushed it off and kissed her sweet face. "Okay," she said. "You had it, mister!" She rolled me over and got on top of me, holding my arms outstretched. "Should I tell your wrestlers that I just pinned you?" We laughed, but she had me stuck in the snow quite well. "I'm no weakling, Coach." She had that beautiful smile. "Say, uncle and I will let you go!"

We rolled around and laughed. Threw snow at each other and laughed. We made snow angels. She said she would come out later and take a picture of the snow angels. That gave her an idea. She went into the house and came back with her cell phone. After the pic of the snow angels we made, she took pictures of the beautiful snowy landscape.

Now, it was selfie time. She snapped pics of silly poses we made in the snow. She wanted to take a pic of her pinning me, but I vetoed that thought. We took turns posing with Snowy, our new friend.

We went inside, and I gave her a pair of sweat clothes and told her to throw the wet clothes in the laundry room. We sat together in our sweat clothes by the fire, drinking hot chocolate.

For lunch, we could not decide between chicken noodle soup or tomato soup. So, we made both. I made us grilled cheese to go with the soup.

We went back to the fire and played cards, rummy, and Uno. We laughed so much during both games. During the Uno game, she had one card left. She put a red 8 on a blue 6. "Hey," I exclaimed. You can't put a red 8 on a blue 6!"

She leaned towards me, "If I give you a big kiss, can I put that card down?" She blinked her eyes and puckered her lips.

"Okay. Bribery will get you everything." I leaned in and gave her a nice kiss. She put her arms in the air, "Yay, I won!"

We were silly all day. We were together all day. We were in the moment.

We decided we should at least call our parents for New Year's. We did not want them to worry. Sam called her folks first. Her mom screamed over the phone when she told her about us. Her dad yelled into the phone, "We've got to meet this guy who finally swept my girl off her feet!" They always worried about her being lonely and working all the time. That sounded familiar.

My parents were also thrilled. I think my mom was crying happy tears. Her son was not alone this year for the holidays. They were on their way in their golf cart to go golfing and have a party after!

We watched a romantic comedy while eating popcorn. We made chocolate chip cookies from scratch. Of course, there was a flour war! After we both had flour on our faces, we had a flour kiss. We heated up a frozen pizza for dinner. Life was good. Life was great again!

Both of us had early mornings the next day. I had Cass's hour, and she had an early shift. We decided that we would rather sleep together that night and get up very early rather than be alone.

We went to bed early, in my king bed. She wore the same tee shirt and shorts. I wore gym shorts and a tee shirt as well. We were fine with that. We were open and could discuss anything. It was decided that lovemaking would come in time. We snuggled together under the covers. It was amazing that with her next to me, I could sleep much better. Sam felt the same way. I think we were made to sleep together. When one of us turned, the other seemed to sense it and turn as well. We were in contact with each other all night.

We both agreed that this had been the best New Year's Day ever! Shell Samuels and Mickey Cassman were starting a wonderful dream, together!

Chapter 29

School resumed on Tuesday, January 2nd. Our next match of the year was scheduled for the next day. Most of the league's wrestling matches were in January and early February. The state required athletes in certain sports to have a minimum amount of practice before their first contest.

The sport of wrestling requires 20 practice days before a wrestler can compete. For that reason, matches do not start until December. Very few matches take place in December, because of holidays. That is why most of the matches take place after January 1.

In order to fit all the schools on the schedule, the league schedules 3 matches a week in January. There is one match on Wednesday because it is a school night. On Friday, a team wrestles two opponents, what is referred to as a "double dual." So, Mayville will have three matches a week.

Mayville was ready, toned, conditioned, and focused! We had our first home match of the new year, on Wednesday, January 3rd, against Riverdale. When I looked up in the bleachers, I saw Sam sitting with

Suzie and the kids. She gave me a smile and a small wave. She knew I was focused.

The gym was packed. I had started a parents' booster club. Their mission was to help support the wrestling program. Coaches must be careful dealing with booster clubs. Some parents want to be *too* involved with their kids in sports. We made it clear from the beginning that I would coach, and they would booster. We would not interfere with each other.

Scotty started out our first home match. When he was announced, he hopped out to the middle of the mat. Pete's two teenage daughters yelled, "Go, Scotty." Scott did not waste much time. He pinned his opponent in 32 seconds! The crowd went crazy. I noticed an older gentleman sitting on the first row of bleachers. He had an artificial leg, walked with a cane, and had a Vietnam Veterans hat on. He clapped and tapped his cane when Scott won.

The rest of the team continued the momentum. We won 52-9. The team was happy but remained focused. We had two more teams on Friday. At the same time we were beating Riverdale on Wednesday, Rockford High School upset Troy at another site.

Rockford had been building their program up and was always dangerous. They seemed like the new powerhouse.

On Friday, we beat Oakwood and Pine Valley, both by over 40 points. Rockford beat Wheatley, who beat us in December. Rockford was the new powerhouse in the league. They were the only undefeated team.

On Wednesday, January 10, we wrestled East Shores and beat them handily, 55-6. It was another home match. That same gentleman, the veteran, was watching. This time he had brought with him a man and a woman. After the match, they introduced themselves to me. The veteran's name is Ed Black. Ed lost his leg in Vietnam. He introduced the other two as Aaron Griffin and Jane Oliver. Aaron and Jane represent the local amputee care clinic. The clinic works with amputees in occupational rehab, as well as getting them back into society. They also have specialists who work with the mental health of amputees.

Ed Black volunteers at the clinic. Ed was so impressed with Scott. He brought Aaron and Jane to watch Scotty wrestle. They were hoping to speak to Scott and his parents. If they were amenable, they would like to know if Scott and his parents could be guest speakers at one of their sessions. I introduced these folks to Scott and his parents. Gage kept listening in, as well.

On Friday, we beat two more schools, Pearson and Central, by huge margins. Our record was 7-1. Rockford had a couple of injuries, which resulted in them losing on Friday to Pine Valley. There were now 3 teams tied for first place in the league; Troy, Rockford, and Mayville.

The team had Saturday and Sunday off. Monday was a day off from school, Martin Luther King Day. I scheduled practice for 12 noon on Monday. I told them to keep their focus. Remember, I said, "*We started a dream!*"

Chapter 30

Sam and I had texted and talked every day. We were able to fit in 4 more sleepovers during those first two weeks of January. Our schedules would not allow us to get together as often as we wanted. However, we knew that, coming into this relationship. We valued our time together. Dr. Morgan was spot on with that assessment.

Sam was not scheduled to work Saturday and Sunday of MLK weekend. We had an opportunity to be together for two days and possibly three nights. It was decided that I would take her up to the cabin. Her first trip to the cabin! Sam was able to get to my double dual match on Friday. After the match, we headed up to the cabin with her backpack in tow. This time she brought her own pjs and toothbrush!

We were both tired, but we wanted to get to the cabin on Friday, so we would not have to drive to the cabin Saturday morning. It was a tedious drive. I was tired, and it was late at night. Sam helped keep me awake. We made it to the cabin safely but were very tired. We had a quick glass of wine. We got into bed, kissed, and snuggled together. We slept soundly.

Saturday was a beautiful day up in the mountains and at the cabin. The sun shone over the snow-covered ground and lake. There are a few birds that do not leave for the winter. The sparrows, blackbirds, and woodpeckers stay around and make beautiful sounds. The geese are alive and soaring overhead. It was a perfect day for Sam and me to relax together.

We had coffee by the fireplace. I made us smoothies with berries and bananas. We bundled up and headed outside.

We took a ride in my jeep and rode around the lake, taking in the sights. "This is a beautiful place, Mick," Sam exclaimed as she looked out the window. "I see why you love to come here."

"It's relaxing," I replied. "This is where I do much of my thinking and reflecting." Sam was still looking out the window, but I could see her smiling and nodding. She probably thought that this was the place that helped me figure life out. She probably thought that this was the place that helped bring her into my life.

After our ride around the lake, I took Sam on a slow ride through the cute little town, where everyone lived their simple life. She smiled and nodded, noticing how life can slow down in a nice little relaxing town like that.

We did some cross-country skiing. Sam had never tried it before, but she caught on quickly. She is a very good athlete.

We built another snow person and named *her* 'snowete.' We told her we would try to match her up with Snowy, and we know all about being fixed up! It was warm enough to build a fire in the fire pit. We roasted hot dogs on sticks and toasted marshmallows, and made smores.

It was a beautiful and relaxing day. We walked hand in hand around the lake. We waived to a few of the neighbors who were up for the weekend. I enjoyed having Sam at my side.

As the sun was getting ready to set, I told her that I had a plan. "I like your plans," she said. We went into the cabin. Grabbed a glass of wine. Sam and I went outside hand in hand. She looked up at me quizzically and smiled. We walked to the edge of the property, one of my favorite places to watch the sunset.

There it was, one of my favorite views. The sunset and the entire horizon lit up in a reddish-orange glow! One of the most beautiful sunsets ever! "Wow," Sam exclaimed with her mouth wide open. She was lost for words. She was lost in the moment like I experienced many times right from this very spot. I grabbed both of her shoulders and turned her towards me. I wanted to tell her something special. I was waiting for the perfect moment. This *was* the perfect moment.

She looked up at me with those beautiful brown eyes. "Shell Samuels, I love you!" I wanted to say more, but I was all choked up. I could see the tears form in her eyes. Then a tear rolled down her cheek toward the cute dimple on her right side. She threw her arms around my neck. "Mickey Cassman," she started and stopped. She sniffed and smiled. "I love you back!"

We slowly leaned toward each other and kissed, with the beautiful sunset sky behind us! This was the first time we told each other that we loved each other. What a beautiful setting for expressing our love. What a picture this would have made.

Chapter 31

Sam and I walked into the cabin with our arms around each other. We sat, looking out the back window, with a glass of wine. We talked candidly about how our love progressed. We got to know and respect each other before we even hugged. When it was time, we kissed. When are feelings grew into a love for the other person, we express that love. "I'm not sure if that's how they draw it up in books," I remarked as we looked out the window.

"Do they have books on how a relationship should progress?" She asked and laughed.

"If not," I replied. "We should write one." We both laughed.

"Listen to us," she laughed. "The *big* experts!" That was hilarious. Two people who were alone for a long time. Two people who were trying to find their way in life. We were laughing at the thought of being experts!

"I will be right back," she said. Sam left for the bedroom. I tended the fire then I stared into the fireplace. I had opened the door to my heart. The love and passion were spilling out like Dr. Morgan said they would. It was a wonderful feeling.

I heard the bedroom door open. I was still in thought. Sam said, "Hey Coach, wanna teach me some wrestling moves?"

I turned around and saw Sam in this see-through nightgown. The only thing she wore under her gown was her panties. Her hair was brushed and lying on her shoulders. She was the sexiest person I have ever seen!

I walked towards her. She took both of my hands in hers and smiled. "Close your eyes," she said. Sam led me into the bedroom, and her walking backward. When we got inside the bedroom, she let go with her right hand and said, "Voila, welcome to my abode!" I opened my eyes, and her right arm showed me the setup. She had turned the bed down. She replaced the bulbs in the two-night table lamps with red bulbs. It was time!

I put both hands on her cheeks and kissed her. I picked her up like a baby and kissed her as I laid her down on the bed. We made out passionately. For the first time, our mouths opened, and our tongues met. Our first French kiss! Our tongues touched each other with the tips. Then our tongues found each other's mouths.

As we passionately kissed, our hands reached up inside each other's tops and rubbed their backs. I moved my right hand to her breasts and softly caressed her breasts. She felt so soft and pure. She sighed and lay on her back with her arms in the air. "Your hands are so soft and smooth," she whispered. I helped her take her nightgown off over her head. She lay there almost naked, such a gorgeous body.

I took off my shirt so we could put our naked chests together. It felt so wonderful. She reached for my shorts and felt the hardness through my shorts. "Wow, someone is excited," she whispered and laughed. Sam pulled my shorts off, then removed her panties. We explored each other's bodies with our hands.

As Sam and I touched and explored, she started to moan and arch… and smile. We continued to touch as the passion grew. We knew it was time. She laid back with both arms up. I got on top of her. I slowly entered her. She arched and moaned, a good moan. I slowly got deeper inside of her. It felt so wonderful. Our movements were slow and deliberate. We were making love.

We rolled over with her on top and me still inside of her. She grabbed my wrists and pinned my arms above me. "Pinned," she whispered. "I won't tell anyone." She smiled. Her body looked so beautiful on top of me. We continued to make love.

We rolled over again, and we kissed as our movements got more intense. I got deeper and more passionate as her arms reached above her, and she made fists around the pillows. She reached down, grabbed the sheets, and made fists. She put her arms out 'spread eagle' position. I put my hands in hers, and we interlaced our fingers. We squeezed our hands, and I knew she was ready to climax. I was ready to explode. "Sam," I said quizzically.

"It's okay," she said, almost out of breath. "I'm protected!"

She had a huge climax and moaned while, at the same time, I released inside of her. Our climaxes were long and thrilling. We both had chills in our arms and throughout our bodies. We started to relax, and I could feel some more. I continued, and we both climaxed again together.

We laid on our backs. I said, "Wow!"

Sam replied, "Double wow!"

I said, "Triple wow!"

She put her head on my chest. "The was the best wow ever! I love you, Mick."

"I love you too, Sam. Good night, dear."

"Good night, my sweetheart."

We covered each other up and fell asleep with our naked bodies against each other. I thought that we would probably never sleep together with our clothes on again!

Chapter 32

When we woke up Sunday morning, it was wonderful waking up to each other. We made love first thing in the morning. We stayed in bed all morning. The morning coffee could wait. We made love and napped and made love some more.

There was nothing else that mattered in our crazy and busy lives. We told each other not to think about tomorrow and work. We decided to stay in the moment. We eventually got out of bed around 12:30. We had on our comfy clothes, and she was wrapped in a blanket because it was a bit chilly. We laughed at how silly we were, like two teenagers having sex for the first time.

Sam confided in me that this was her first time. She had dated but never had a relationship. She said that she was old school and wanted to save herself. My smile could not have been bigger!

We huddled under her blanket by the back window and looked out at the beautiful land and lake again. We knew this was a weekend we would never forget. We did not feel like eating, so we just snacked a bit. I built a fire in the fireplace.

Sam went into the bedroom for a bit. I went into the guest bedroom and brought the mattress and bedding out in front of the fireplace. I lit a candle and set it on the coffee table. I dimmed the lights. I hurried to the bedroom door, and when she came out, I said, "Now it's my turn. Close your eyes."

I led her with both hands around the couch and over to the mattress in front of the fireplace. "Voila, my dear!" She opened her eyes and laughed. "You have way too many clothes on for this next activity," I joked.

"Okay, Coach." We got naked and got under the covers. We made love in front of the fireplace… over and over and over!

We debated when to head home. Sam had to be at the hospital at 6 am on Monday. I had practice at 12 noon, the MLK holiday. We figured it was better to head back to town Sunday night rather than make the ride in the morning. Either way, we were intent on sleeping together Sunday night.

We decided to pack up the cabin and drive into town tonight. Halfway down the mountain, we ran across a young couple stuck in a ditch on the side of the road. There was a crying baby in her car seat in the back seat. We stopped to help. Our plan was for the woman to get behind the wheel, and the two guys would try to push the car out. Sam offered to hold the little girl.

The woman got behind the wheel. We started to push but noticed that she had the front wheels turned. "Straighten the wheels," I yelled as I made circular motions with my finger. We got the car rocking back and forth. One final forward, then back, and with our pushing, we got it out onto the road.

"Whew," I said as I started brushing off. The man came over to me and started to pull out his wallet, "let me pay you, sir."

I put my hand up in a stop position. "No way." I looked at his wife, who was still stressed. Then I looked at their baby daughter. Sam had her calmed down, and the baby was cooing at her. What a wonderful sight. I shook his hand and put my other hand on his shoulder. "Just take care of your beautiful family, son. That is how you can pay me back." The four of us chatted for a bit. We went our separate ways.

On the drive home, I looked at Sam. "You looked quite natural with that child." She did not respond. Sam hugged my arm and put her head on my shoulder.

It made sense for us to sleep at her house because she had an earlier start. When she would leave for work, I would head back to my house. She said I could sleep in rather than get up early with her. I said, "No way. I want to get up with my sweetie."

We went to bed at her place Sunday night of MLK weekend. We were naked, which was our new wardrobe when we were in bed together. We made love and fell right to sleep. When her alarm went off in the morning, we rolled over and had our "morning rollover," as we called it. We made love.

Sam and I said, "I love you" to each other. She went to work, and I went to my house. The love from our hearts stayed together.

The practice was spirited and intense. We knew we were in a 3-way tie for first place. The other two teams were Troy and Rockford. Wheatley had beaten us back in December. They lost to Troy and Rockford. We were ahead of Wheatley in the standings. I was working on the side with our heavyweight, Bubby Chance. Bubby was trying hard, but he had not won a match all year. I was trying to teach him a new move.

I told him that when heavyweight wrestlers are on top of their opponents, they like to hang their arms around the waist. Most heavyweights can get caught in a roll and get reversed. A reversal in wrestling is when the bottom wrestler gets out from the bottom and gets on top of his opponent. There are many moves to accomplish this. One of those moves is the roll.

I was teaching Bubby a special kind of roll. It is called a wrist roll and leg lever. The bottom man grabs the opponent's wrist and starts to roll. Most top wrestlers will stop the roll by bracing their legs. I taught Bubby to hook his toe under the opponent's leg and kick it over. I call it the leg lever.

Bubby and I practiced it over and over. He was getting it quite well. Later in practice, he was wrestling Neil. Neil was on top. Bubby caught him in the wrist roll and leg lever and rolled Neil to his back. Neil struggled under Bubby's weight but eventually used his strength to get off his back. I blew the whistle ending the practice match. Neil stood up and yelled at me. "Hey Cass, what did you teach this guy? I couldn't stop that move! You turned him into an animal!"

Bubby gave me a thumbs-up. The team laughed. They were all behind Bubby. Bubby was trying so hard. They were encouraging him every day!

Chapter 33

Sam and I texted back and forth on Monday. We were in love! I had the remainder of the day off because it was the MLK holiday. I suggested that I go to her house and make her a steaming hot dinner for when she came home. I told her that I would prepare the meal and she could text me when she left the hospital. I would then start the meal.

She responded, saying that sounded awesome. Then she surprised me and texted, **bring a change of clothes and toiletries, sailor. I'm not letting you leave.** Thus, started our nights of sleeping over at the other's house. We both knew that a night alone would pale compared to being together. When I roll over in the middle of the night, it is wonderful to find her next to me. Waking up next to her is a pleasure every time. Sam feels the same way.

We did not necessarily have to make love. Just being together is a pleasure. Of course, early on in this relationship, we acted like two horny teenagers!

That evening at dinner, she told me that she took Suzie aside and confided in her about our intimacy. Suzie was so ecstatic. Suzie said she was jealous. Sorry, Pete!

There was girl talk. Sam was respectful of our relationship and kept the intimate details private. Sam imitated how Suzie had held her hands in the air about six inches apart. Suzie asked, "So how big?" Sam responded to her, "I'm not telling….but!" Then Sam spread her hands wide apart! They had girl fun! Sam and I laughed for a long time.

Tuesday morning was awesome. We woke up together. Had our teenage thing. Then I made us coffee. We kissed and told each other, "I love you." We went in different directions with smiles on our faces and love in our hearts.

Tuesday was a typical day in my Phys. Ed classes. I was itching to get my team back into action on Wednesday. I could not wait to "unleash" them on another opponent. The team was fired up in practice. I think I created a monster!

At dinner that evening, Sam and I discussed how exciting it was to come home to each other. Spending all night together. Waking up with each other. Our relationship was a release for each of us. Our love and our relationship turned our lives around. We had a partner to talk to, to lean on, and to share with.

Sam and I were not alone anymore. We both mentioned that before we met and we lived by ourselves, it did not feel lonely. Then, we met each other. We got to know each other. We spent more time together. Now, when we are apart, it feels lonely.

Dr. Morgan said that she was proud of the work that I did. Developing our youth. Volunteering. All of that is wonderful. She said that in order to maintain that caring and helping, I had to take care of myself *first*. "You must fill up your cup first before caring for and helping others," was one of her sayings. My cup is currently full to the brim! Thanks to Shell Samuels!

Chapter 34

Wednesday, our match was against Fairview High School. It was a home match. Before the match, Scott told me that he, Gage, and his parents had visited a clinic over the weekend. They talked to amputees, mainly children and their parents. Some were expected to attend the match tonight. When we entered the gym, I could see the amputees and their parents proudly sitting in the bleachers. Ed Black, our Vietnam amputee veteran, was sitting with them.

That evening we were on the verge of completing something that is rare in wrestling. There is a team scoring scale in wrestling. If you defeat an opponent by scoring more points than him, you earn 3 points for your team. There is a sliding scale as the difference in points becomes greater. If a wrestler outscores his opponent by 8-11 points, then they earn 4 team points. This is referred to as a 'major decision.' A difference of 12-14 points earns him a 'superior decision,' 5 points for the team. If the wrestler beats his opponent by 15 or more points, it is called a 'technical pin,' which results in 6 team points. If a wrestler pins his opponent's shoulders to the mat for a count of two seconds, it is a pin; 6 team points.

Scotty started out by pinning his opponent in the first match, 98 lb. wt. class. Six points for the team. Bo Bennett was next up in the 105 lb. wt. class. Bo pinned his opponent. Six more points for the team. Leo Carter, at 112 lb. wt. class, pinned his opponent. Six more points for the team.

Next was Jazz, then Tycz, and Logan, all pins. Gage is a stud and pinned his opponent in the first 30 seconds. Lucas at 145 lbs., Jake at 155 lbs., and William at 167 lbs. all pinned their opponents. Neil just mauled his opponent and pinned him in the first period.

Going into Bubby's heavyweight match, every wrestler from Mayville had pinned their opponent. We were working on a perfect score! Bubby had not won a match all year. The team talked to him and encouraged him before he went on the mat.

Bubby's opponent was one of their better wrestlers. He took Bubby down to the mat for 2 points. At the end of the first period, Bubby was losing 4-1. Bubby started the second period on top but quickly got reversed. The score was 6-1. I could tell Bubby's opponent was getting tired. I cupped my hands around my mouth and yelled, "Bubby, your move."

Instinctively, Bubby grabbed his opponent's wrist, which was around his waist. Bubby took the wrist and did a wrist roll. His opponent started going over but caught himself with his leg. Bubby then used the 'leg lever' move he had just learned and practiced.

Bubby was able to kick his opponent's legs over and complete the roll. Bubby landed on top of his opponent, who was on his back. Our team went wild. Bubby put all his weight on his opponent and used the half-Nelson; arm behind the head. His opponent struggled until he ran out of gas.

The referee slapped the mat, indicating Bubby had pinned his opponent! Bubby won his first match ever. I have a team sportsmanship rule. I do not allow the wrestlers to show off or overly celebrate while on the wrestling mat. I tell them that they would embarrass themselves, their school, and their family. Putting their arms in the air and feeling good is acceptable.

Bubby put his arms in the air in celebration. He helped his opponent up, and they hugged. The sportsmanship tradition in our league was for the wrestler to go to the opposing coach and shake their hand. Bubby ran to the other coach and shook his hand. Bubby came running over to our side of the mat with a huge smile. He was ready to jump into my arms. I said, "Oh boy!"

Neil pushed me with his shoulder. "I got this, Cass," he shouted. Bubby jumped into Neil's arms. Neil is the strongest person I have ever met. He almost got knocked over but stayed on his feet. The team crowded around Bubby and kept slapping him on his back and rustling his hair. I saw Bubby's mom in the bleachers wiping tears from her eyes with a Kleenex. We gave the other team a cheer and walked across the mat shaking hands.

We had completed a perfect 72-0 score. Rare in high school wrestling. This team was scary good! I would not want to be an opposing coach against these guys!

Chapter 35

Sam and I tried to spend every night together at one of our homes. Periodically we would take additional clothes to the other's house. We made every effort to sleep together every night. On rare occasions, we would have to be apart. Sometimes she would draw a rare overnight shift.

Being alone, without my loving partner, was lonely. It was amazing how feelings about loneliness changed for us in our lives.

On Friday of this week, we wrestled the Cartersville and Wayne High Schools. We beat them both by over a 50-point margin! Mayville was on fire. Our team record was 10-1. We were tied for first with Troy and Rockford, who had the same 10-1 record.

The following Wednesday, we defeated Wade High School by another huge score. On Friday, we took care of two more schools; Rivergrove and Rosedale. 13-1 record.

After the match, Sam came out of the bleachers and stood next to Suzie. A man, looking to be in his 60s, started talking to them. Sam walked over with him. The man shook my hand aggressively. I did not recognize him. "Coach, my name is Duke McGovern. I understand that you have a booster club that supports your team. I would like to donate a substantial amount to your booster club."

"Thank you very much, Mr. McGovern," still shaking his hand. I thought I noticed that he was sitting with the fans for Rosedale. "Do you mind if I ask? I saw you….."

"Say no more, Coach. Yes, I went to Rosedale many years ago," he laughed. "More years than I wish to admit. I always follow their wrestling program. All my boys wrestled there. I don't have any on the team now, but I still follow them." I looked puzzled. "Let me get to the point. You and this pretty woman here rescued my son, daughter-in-law, and granddaughter, when they went off the road. It was up in the mountains during Martin Luther King weekend. It was stormy and dangerous. My son tried to pay you, but you wouldn't take any money. I really appreciate you saving their lives during that terrible storm. That's is why I'm paying it forward to your program." He was starting to choke up. "You saved their lives!" He took out a handkerchief and wiped his face. Sam gave him a big hug. I thanked him, gave him a hug, and said, "Bless you." I introduced Mr. McGovern to our booster club president.

The following Wednesday, we hosted Rockford in our gym. Both teams were 13-1, tied for first place in the league. The gym was packed.

Scott, Gage, and their parents visited pediatric patients in the cancer wing of the hospital. We were aware that some of these patients were given permission from the hospital to leave to attend tonight's match. We roped off a section in the bleachers for the kids and their families, as well as the people from the amputee clinic. Mr. Black, our Vietnam amputee friend, has not missed a match since his first visit. He even attends the away matches in other gyms.

Scott seemed more motivated than ever. He hopped out onto the mat and shook hands with his opponent. When the whistle blew, it was amazing how quickly he could move around on the mat. He is also a smart wrestler and learned more and more moves. He practices hard. You could see his extreme progress from week to week.

Scotty controlled his opponent from the opening whistle. He was leading 9-0 when he finally turned his opponent over and pinned him. Six points for the team. Mayville was not to be intimidated by Rockford's record.

Scotty set the tone, and the rest of the team followed with amazing wrestling. I knew they were motivated; however, I was so impressed with their tenacity. With every win, you could feel the momentum build. Mayville defeated Rockford 45-9! The news reporters, who were there, were stunned. Sports reporters had predicted a close team score. They did not know the Mayville wrestling team the way I knew this team.

Friday of this week was the last week of the original schedule. We wrestled the Walnut Grove and Windemere High Schools. We beat both schools by over a 50-point margin. Our record stood at 16-1.

We had one match remaining. It was our makeup against Troy from the cancellation in December due to the snowstorm. Both teams were 16-1, tied for first place. The match was rescheduled for the following Wednesday at Troy's gymnasium.

I suggested to the team to take Saturday and Sunday off to rest. We will come back on Monday and Tuesday to prepare. Gage and Scott invited the team members to their house on Saturday. They would lift, jog, and watch some sports on TV. They also planned to watch some "Rocky" movies for motivation.

I have fallen in love with this team. Another door has opened in my heart. The love for the hard work and dedication that these young athletes were displaying. Their comradery was outstanding. There were times like this that humbled me.

Sam and I were able to have a weekend without work. We went to the cabin and relaxed. At least I tried to relax. Sam could feel my angst and anxiety. Sam and I discussed the big match coming up. She listened to me. She was a great listener. She was a wonderful sounding board.

I was going over every individual match in my mind. I knew Troy, the opponent. I had coached all of them, some since youth wrestling.

I knew that once the wrestler stepped onto the mat, there was not much I could do to help him. I always believed that a coach's best coaching was during practices. A coach's job is to prepare the wrestler before he steps on the mat. I wanted to make sure that I covered everything on Monday and Tuesday to get them prepared.

I am so thankful that I have my loving partner with me. I looked over at her and said, "I love you. Thank you for being you."

"You're welcome, Coach." She replied. "It's easy being me when you are who you are! I love you. I love you to bits!"

Practices on Monday and Tuesday were intense and focused. The entire school was buzzing. Larry Bagwell, the Athletic Director, ordered a bus for the students to attend the match at Troy.

Mayville has not had many championship teams in their history in any sport. They have never finished near the top in wrestling. The entire town of Mayville was talking about the big match. People were planning to show up early to get a seat in the bleachers. It was exciting. It was fun to be a part of.

After practice on Tuesday, I felt the team was ready. I told them to go home and get a good night's sleep. I am not sure if any of us would sleep much on Tuesday night!

Chapter 36

It is Tuesday night, before the big match. I am lying in bed with Sam in our usual attire - nothing. We enjoy our naked bodies touching each other.

I was staring at the ceiling, deep in thought. Sam had her head lying on my chest. I was rubbing her back. "I'm proud of you, Mick," she said in a low tone.

"Thanks. What for?" I kept staring at the ceiling.

"You molded these boys into a wonderful team," she complimented. "I'm not just talking skill-wise. You taught them sportsmanship, team unity, and respect. They look up to you, Mick. You are a great role model. You have turned these boys into young men." Sam and I have had many discussions about the team. She is beginning to know how my mind works.

"I have so much confidence in this team tomorrow," she continued as I kept staring at the ceiling. I was not staring at anything in particular. Just staring. "But win, lose, or draw, your accomplishments throughout the year have been amazing. Those accomplishments cannot be overshadowed by one match." I knew she was correct. If the season were to end today, the season would be an outstanding success. These young men have grown up so much this year. They worked hard to get to where they were.

"You are correct, my dear," I finally broke my silence. "The team started a dream. We are almost there!"

We kissed good night, as we always do. We told each other, "I love you." Sam fell asleep on my chest. I kept rubbing her back and went back to my thoughts.

Wednesday, during Cass hour, the match is all that everyone talked about. During morning announcements, Karen Fryer, the Principal, reminded the students what time the booster buses would leave. The school decided to pay for the buses. Students had to sign up.

Most of the sports editors from the different towns had predicted Troy would win in a close match. The Troy Times predicted a resounding win for Troy. The only favorable comment was from our local paper, the Mayville Mailer. The sports editor predicted that we had an outside chance to pull an upset! Gee, thanks!

As a team, we went through our regular routine. We arrived at the school and took a walk around the gymnasium. I wanted the wrestlers to get used to the surroundings. Everything came back to me from my last four years at Troy. There were many memories. Now I was an opposing coach.

The wrestlers got into their singlets and warmups. They sat around, trying to get into the moment. I walked into the locker room. All eyes were on me. I started my pre-match speech.

"I am so proud of each and every one of you," I started. "We have come so far as a team. Regardless of tonight's outcome…."

Suddenly Scott stood up and said, "Excuse me, Coach." I never had my pre-match speech interrupted before. Scott was normally a quiet kid. He was starting to come out of his shell. He remained standing and continued. "Coach Cass, I owe everything that happened to me this year to you. You have given me a purpose in life. I have a leg missing, but you have made me whole again. We started a dream!" He finished emphasizing that statement! He remained standing.

Jake stood up. "Cass, I'm still wrestling because of your influence. You helped me to see how compassion during the holidays can make people smile. You demonstrated a sense of caring for my family and other kids and families. You made us a family! We started a dream!" Jake's turn to emphasize that statement! Jake remained standing.

Tycz stood up. "Cass, you helped me to be able to read when no one else seemed to care." He started sobbing, "I love to read. I just finished my first book last weekend! We started a dream!" Tycz remained standing also.

Leo stood up. "Cass, you, or the shoe fairy bought me shoes when my family couldn't afford them. It wasn't about the shoes. It taught me to help those less fortunate. We started a dream!" Leo also stayed on his feet.

My eyes were really tearing up. One by one, the wrestlers were expressing their feelings about our journey towards our dream. They were also sharing the lessons that the sport of wrestling had taught them in life.

Bubby stood up. "Cass, I was a nobody. I'm no longer the fat kid in school with no friends. You made me feel like a 'somebody.' I might even have a date for next weekend. Bubby raised his fist high and stood tall as he shouted out, "We started a dream!"

Gage and Neil stood up together. "Cass," Gage started. "You brought us up near the mountain top." Neil continued. "Now it's up to us to reach the top of that mountain." He pounded his mighty fist into his open hand. "We plan to crush anyone who wants to stop us from reaching that goal." Gage and Neil together said, "We started a dream!"

The rest of the varsity team stood up and joined hands in a circle. They all looked at me. Neil looked around the circle. "What did we do?" He shouted. Together they all said, "We started a dream!"

I joined the circle between Neil and Scott. I looked around and said, "You are all correct. We started a dream!"

Jazz, who has never said more than 2 words all season, said, "Just a second, Coach." He took his earbuds out of his ears. He unplugged the headphones from his iPod. Everyone looked at him. Suddenly, the British rock group 'Queen' started playing. It was entitled "We Will Rock You."

The song starts with foot stamping, "'boom, boom, boom. Boom, boom, boom. We will, we will rock you.'" The team picked up the beat, clapping their hands and stomping their feet. Then they started singing, "We will, we will rock you. We will, we will rock you!"

I wiped my tears with the back of my hand. I said in a choking voice, "Let's finish this dream!"

We turned around and ran out of the locker room into the gym.

Chapter 37

The gymnasium was packed. Standing room only. Sam had taken the night off to attend. She sat with Suzie and the kids. The section roped off for the amputee clinic guests, as well as the cancer patients, was jam-packed with kids and parents. Ed Black was there with his cane and his family. Scotty had his own cheering section, this reserved section, plus Pete's two older daughters!

I was surprised to see a local tv station there. The administrators from both schools were present. Assistant Superintendent Bill Handley was there. He was the person who broke the news to me that I was being transferred. Charlie Quinn, the head football coach from Mayville, was in the stands. I was really surprised to see Dr. Helen Morgan in attendance. Duke McGovern, the gentleman from Rosedale who, donated money to our boosters because Sam and I rescued his family was in the stands. He was smiling at our team.

The Junior Varsity matches take place before the varsity. On this night, the Mayville JV team beat Troy's JV team. Our JV team finished the year undefeated. That looms well for the future. It is also a tribute to the fact that we all practice together. Our JV wrestlers have been sparring with wrestlers like Gage, Neil, and the rest of the varsity. It only makes them better.

Both teams are lined up on the side of the mat. When the wrestlers are announced, they go to the middle of the mat. They shake hands with their opponent, then return to the lineup. Scott, being the first weight class, was announced first. He looked focused. They all looked focused. Scott and his opponent shook hands in the middle of the mat, returned to their respective sides of the mat, and started warming up.

The heavyweights were the last to be announced. The coaches were announced. Andy and I went in front of the scorer's table and shook hands. We did a friendly embrace. I brought Andy into the Troy program, and we worked well together. Andy spoke first. "You did a great job with that team, Cass. Good luck tonight."

"Thanks," I was short. I think he could see the focus in my eyes. "Good luck."

It was showtime!

Scotty was the first match of the night. Right from the opening whistle, he was slick. He moved in and out, up and down. He spun around for a quick takedown, 2-0. He put his opponent on his back a few times and earned extra points. If Scott could pin his man, it would be a great start.

Scott pulled out all the stops. He used moves I didn't know he knew! He wore his man down. Eventually, he turned him over and pinned his opponent. 6-0 Mayville.

Bo was next. He was up against a tough opponent. Bo kept it close but lost by a point in the last 5 seconds. Team score, 6-3 Mayville. I had preached to the kids that even if you lose, you can help the team win by not giving up too many points. If a wrestler gets beat by a point or two, it is much better than getting pinned.

Leo was next in the 112 lb. wt. class. He also had a tough opponent. Leo wrestled one of his better matches of the year. He was ahead against a tough opponent. Leo got taken down just at the buzzer to lose, but only 3 team points. The team score was 6-6. I am guessing that Coach Andy was hoping to pick up some extra points in those last two weight classes. Bo and Leo did their jobs by keeping it close.

Jazz was next. He was so excited he almost forgot to take his earbuds out! Jazz is tall and thin and very wiry. He makes it difficult for his opponent. Jazz was behind towards the end. He used his wiry body to get a reversal. He was still behind. He used his long arms and long legs to get his man in a cradle move. He took his opponent to the mat in a pinning move. The crowd went wild. Time ran out, but Jazz got extra points for putting his opponent on his back. Jazz won. Team score, 9-6, Mayville.

Our next two wrestlers, Tycz at 126 lbs. and Logan at 132 lbs., had twin brothers as opponents. The twins were seniors and had wrestled since the youth program. They had much more experience than Tycz and Logan. Tycz and Logan wrestled the best I ever saw them wrestle. They both lost by one point. One point is a darn close match. I am sure Andy expected more from the twins. With those two wins, the team score was 9-12, Troy.

Gage Alan was next, at 138 lbs. Gage is a stud, strong. He is also one of the faster wrestlers on our team. He is a leg rider, which is a move from the top position. Gage's opponent was no match for Gage. Gage wore him down and pinned him. Team score, 15-12, Mayville.

Lucas, at 145 lbs., was one of our quiet wrestlers. He has improved all year. He wrestled very well but lost a close match to a much more experienced wrestler. Team score, 15-15.

Jake, at 155 lbs., and William, at 167 lbs., also wrestled twins. Both twins from Troy are well-built. They both have won most of their matches this year. Jake wrestled his best match of the year and pulled off a huge upset, winning 6-5! 3 points for Mayville. The other twin was so upset he went out there and beat William by a pin. 6 points for Troy. The team score stands at 18-21, Troy.

Now it was time for my stud, Neil Ellis, 177 lbs. Neil is probably the strongest wrestler in the league. Neil shot a takedown and picked his opponent off the mat. He carried him to the middle of the mat with the crowd on their feet. Neil brought him down to the mat and muscled him over to his back. Neil pinned his opponent in the first period. Team score, 24-21, Mayville.

Everyone knew the situation. The last match of the evening was Buster Smythe, the senior from Troy, against Bubby Chance from Mayville. Buster was the best heavyweight in the league. He had one loss all year; he was sick that day and only lost by one point. Buster was big and strong. He was also the hero in Troy's championship match the year prior.

Bubby had only won a few matches all year. If Buster wins a close match, he will earn 3 team points, and the team score will be a tie. We would tie for the championship. If Buster pinned Bubby or won by a huge margin, Troy would win and repeat as league champions.

Buster was overpowering. He could smell victory. He took Bubby down to the mat early, 2-0. Then Buster turned Bubby over on his back. The Troy crowd was yelling, "Buster, Buster!" They were looking for a pin. Bubby was able to bridge his body up and get his arm through and roll over to his stomach. Buster got more points. He led 5-0. The first period ended with Buster leading 5-0.

The second period started with Bubby starting on top and Buster on the bottom. At the whistle, Buster got to his feet, 1 point. Buster took Bubby down to the mat, score now 8-0. That was enough for a major win, which is 4 team points, and would give Troy the win and the championship. They went out of bounds. Buster looked at coach Andy. Andy said to just hang on to him, and they win.

Buster decided to go for more points. He turned Bubby over, and it would have been a pin, but Bubby inched his body so one of his shoulders slid out of bounds. Still 3 more points. Buster was comfortably ahead 11-0. The period ended, one more period to go.

Coach Andy had his fists in the air. He could smell victory. What he did not realize was Buster was getting tired. Because of Bubby's weight, it is tiring wrestling him. I could see Buster breathing hard. We had worked very hard all year at conditioning. The Mayville wrestlers had more stamina than any other team because of our conditioning program.

Before the third period, Bubby looked at his teammates. He was thinking, all that practice, all the hard work! Then Jazz, with his headphones on, starts tapping his feet to the Queen song, "We will rock you!" The rest of the team started tapping their feet to the song. They were not listening, but they knew the rhythm. Boom, boom, boom. Boom, boom, boom.

Bubby slapped himself awake. He looked at me. We both knew that Buster was getting tired. Time for "the move!" The third period started, and sure enough, Buster felt tired just decided to hang on to Bubby and ride out the win. Bubby went for it. He grabbed Buster's wrist and started the wrist roll. Buster almost went over but caught himself with his leg. Bubby used the leg lever and kicked Buster's legs over. The crowd went wild. Bubby had Buster on his back. He locked him up in the half-Nelson hold. Bubby put all his weight on Buster. The referee was down on the mat, looking at Buster's shoulders. If both shoulders were on the mat for 2 seconds, it would be a pin. Buster let out a scream, trying to get out. Bubby had a determined look on his face. His face was turning red, and he squeezed.

Finally, Buster ran out of steam. His shoulders sank to the mat. The referee slapped the mat. A pin for Bubby! Final score Mayville 30-Troy 21! I cannot remember exactly everything that happened at that moment. Bubby helped Buster up, and they hugged. Buster came over to shake my hand. "Great match, Buster," I said. "Thanks, Coach." He still called me coach.

Bubby ran over to Andy. He quickly shook Andy's hand and ran back over to our side of the mat. This time Neil and Jake got behind me, and Neil said, "He's all yours this time, Cass!" Bubby came flying into my arms. Neil and Jake saved me. We were all jumping around like little kids! The team picked me up on their shoulders. I reached down and touched the hands of every wrestler. This was truly a team win. Even those who lost kept the score close, which helped with the team scoring.

Cheerleaders and students were throwing confetti. It was raining happiness! Sam found me in the mix and had tears in her eyes. She kissed me and said, "Congrats, Coach!" The boys all went, "Ohhhh!" Gage sang, "Coach has a girlfriend!" There was laughter and joy for our team. Suzie gave me a kiss on the cheek. The boys again went, "Ohhhh!"

There were congrats from everyone, parents, administrators, and fans. Ed Black and Duke McGovern came over and shook my hand.

Sam tapped me on the shoulder and pointed to where Pete's older daughters, Kaeli and Maris, were talking to Scotty and giggling! Sam and I busted up laughing. Then Scott took the girls over to meet the amputees and the cancer patients. Wow!

Sam and I saw Bubby talking to a girl. Neil was talking to two girls, which made us laugh. Gage was with two girls, as well.

Dr. Morgan was leaving. When she saw me, she waved. I held up a finger, asking her to wait. I took Sam over and introduced her to Dr. Morgan. Sam said, "Is it okay to hug you?" "Of course, dear," she answered. Sam put her arms around Dr. Morgan's neck and said, "Thank you so much for what you did for Mick and for us!" Dr. Morgan looked at me and winked. "I see what you mean, Mickey. She is a keeper!" then she left.

No one wanted to leave the gym. We felt like staying there all night. My old custodian friend from Troy, Joe, waved. I did not want to make his job tougher. I told the team to start getting ready. It was going to be a fun bus ride home!

Chapter 38

Just like a year ago, the bus ride home after the championship was fun. There was teasing back and forth. It made me smile. Gage yelled to Bubby, "Why did you wait so long to pin him, Bubs?" "It was to impress the girls," Bubby replied. Everyone said, "Booo!"

"Hey, Jazz," Scotty yelled. "What's your real name?" Jazz stood up and shyly said, "Mortimere!" "Keep the name Jazz," Jake yelled. Jake had one of the biggest upsets of the night. He and Bubby.

When we were halfway home, Jazz stood up. "I need everyone's attention," he announced. When everyone was quiet, he took his earbuds out. He turned up his iPod. It was the rest of the Queen song. "We are the champions." We sang it all the way home, including the bus driver.

"We are the champions, my friends. And we'll keep fighting till the end. We are the champions; we are the champions. No time for losers, 'cause we are the champions of the world!"

Pete and I enjoyed our "wrestling family." In many ways, they are our family away from home. The only seniors on the team are Jake and Neil. They will be truly missed. When you really connect with your athletes, it is like losing a son when they graduate.

When we were close to the school, I stood up and asked to be heard. The singing stopped, and all eyes were on me. "Gentlemen, I'm not going to say a great job tonight; you already know that. I'm going to tell you to savor this moment. Savor this team, these friendships, this entire year. Back in December, we started a dream. Tonight, we reached that dream. Take that with you in life as you start new dreams. Be with your families tonight. Thank them for the sacrifice that they gave for you, so you could reach this dream."

"We won tonight because of hard work and perseverance. That's another lesson you can take with you in life. Remember, this was a team win. We didn't just win because some of our guys got pins for us. We also won because the other guys wrestled their best. This was a true team win. A "family" win! I love all of you guys!"

Neil yelled from the back, "Hey guys, what did we do in December?" They all said, "We started a dream!"

Sam waited for me in the parking lot. When I came out and saw her, I remarked, "This is a nice surprise. Now, I want to take you home and show you some moves!"

She laughed, "You had better watch out, cowboy. I was paying attention tonight, and I learned a few moves."

I put my arms around her, "then let's go home and continue our dream."

When we got to my place, we went straight to bed to… celebrate!

Chapter 39

The season was over for the junior varsity. I would still see them around school and in phys. ed. class. The varsity wrestlers competed in the Divisional tournament. A wrestler had to place in the top four of their weight class in order to move on to the Sectional tournament.

Scott, Bo, Jazz, Tycz, Gage, Jake, William, Neil, and even Bubby placed in the top four of their weight class. Nine out of twelve wrestlers advanced to the Sectional tournament.

The Sectional tournament is much tougher. The winner of each weight class goes to the state tournament. Scott, Gage, and Neil took first in their weight class and qualified to wrestle the next week in the state tournament. Jake wrestled well and just lost by a point in the finals and missed qualifying. Mayville will be represented by three wrestlers in the state tournament. Mayville has never had a state champion.

Scott, Gage, and Neil trained hard. I told them that in the state tournament, all opponents would be tough. Conditioning and stamina are important. All three got together and started their new dream.

Scott was very impressive. Cameras flashed every time he wrestled. Scott Alan became the first state champion for Mayville in the 98 lb. wt. class. He also became the first one-legged wrestler to win a state championship in our state.

Gage was next. Gage was very determined. He is very intelligent, and you can see him calculate all his moves. In the finals, he wrestled the returning state champion from a year ago. It was a back-and-forth match. Both wrestlers were on their feet, tied with 16 seconds to go. Gage found an opening and took his opponent down to the mat. Gage held him down and became Mayville's second state champion. Gage is a junior.

Neil was warming up for his final match at 177 lb. wt. class. I saw Scott and Gage with him, encouraging him. Neil came out and just mauled his opponent. Neil pinned his opponent in the second period. Mayville had three state champions!

Our end-of-the-year banquet was so much fun. Sam and Suzie sat with us at the head table. Sam was so ravishingly beautiful that I had trouble keeping the fathers' attention on my speech!

I told a few jokes and gave a synopsis of the season. I thanked many people. I especially thanked the parents who sacrificed for their sons. I wanted the wrestlers to understand what parents go through during the season, including all the late dinners after practice.

The booster club had sponsored some awards. After the season we just experienced, how do you award a most valuable or most improved? It is very difficult. I let the wrestlers vote with a paper ballot.

Nate (Bubby) Chance was voted the most improved wrestler. Neil Ellis was voted the most valuable wrestler.

Sam was able to pull strings so that we could go to Florida during Easter break and meet my parents. They just loved Sam. How could they not?

We rode in the golf cart with them. Sam and my dad danced the electric slide together. We golfed and played pickleball with my folks. Mom and Sam went shopping together… and often!

Mom and Dad were head over heels for Sam. They could see how happy I was in life. Mom said to me, "Mickey, honey, that girl is a real gem. You had better keep her close. I see all the old guys around here checking her out!" We laughed hard.

Dad pulled me aside and said, "Mick, it's time to make an honest woman out of Sam. If you don't marry her, I just might!" Dad and I laughed over beers. It was wonderful to have my parents' approval. I had met Sam's family. They were all very supportive of our relationship. Her parents and sisters could see the twinkle in her eyes when she looked at me.

After the school year ended, Sam's birthday was approaching. I told her to get dressed for a romantic night out. I took her down to the boat dock. I scheduled a private boat ride. There was a table set up on the deck with flowers and a bottle of wine. I hired a guitar player to play soft romantic music. It was a beautiful setting. I waited until the sun was setting and that beautiful reddish-orange glow in the sky appeared. I proposed marriage to the woman who turned my life around. The woman who became my partner and best friend. The woman who I wanted to spend the rest of my life with.

I asked Sam to start a new dream with me. I asked her to start a dream of a family and living together for the remainder of our lives.

Sam was crying so hard she had trouble saying the words, "Yes, of course, I will marry you, Mickey Cassman!" We kissed, cried, and laughed together.

Shell Samuels and Mickey Cassman *started a new dream...* *together!*

All our dreams can come true if we have the courage to pursue

them

Walt Disney

The End

Epilogue

Scott Alan went on to become a four-time state wrestling champion. He went on to college and graduated with a degree in engineering. He started his own technology company, which works on developing mobility-related bionics. Scott dated Kaeli for a bit. After high school, they went their separate ways. Scott continues to volunteer at rehab centers. He also visits pediatric cancer patients and donates a substantial amount of money to cancer research. Scott was inducted into the state wrestling Hall of Fame. Scott is happily married and has two children; a boy named Mickey and a girl named Sam.

Bo Bennett continued to wrestle into college. He is a successful high school wrestling coach.

Leo Carter is married and lives comfortably with his family and three dogs. He has a display case, displaying his first pair of wrestling shoes from the 'wrestling fairy.'

Jazz Cyrcle started his own rock band. He travels around the country, playing concerts. Many times, he will open his show with the Queen songs, "We will rock you" and "We Are the Champions."

Tycz Brock continued to read. He went to college a became a reading teacher. He has written many books geared toward helping children to learn to read.

Gage Alan became a two-time state champion. He decided not to wrestle in college but rather pursue his academics. Gage earned his Ph.D. in organic chemistry. He was hired right out of graduate school and is happily married. Gage and Scott still debate over strategies and penalties when they watch football together.

Logan, Lucas, and William continued wrestling in high school, and all three ended their senior year with outstanding records.

Jake Grayson went on to wrestle at a junior college. He became a high school guidance counselor and is a successful high school wrestling coach. Jake posts motivational signs around his locker room regarding reaching their dreams. Jake also runs a huge Toys for Tots program around the holidays.

Neil Ellis went on to have a successful football career at a Division-2 college. He earned his degree in business and ran a successful engineering firm. Neil also travels the country, giving motivational speeches.

Nate (Bubby) Chance had a successful senior year in wrestling. He was a divisional and sectional champion. He went to the state tournament and finished third in the state. Bubby was asked to go to the prom every year. His senior year, he was voted prom king!

Mickey and Sam had a beautiful wedding on a huge boat. They timed the ceremony to have the sunset and beautiful reddish-orange glow in the horizon as the background. At the wedding reception, Mickey, Sam, and both sets of parents danced the electric slide together! Anyone and everyone were invited to the wedding! There was joy all around. Two lonely souls were coming together! One of their wedding songs was "I'll Stop the World and Melt With You" by Modern English.

They sold Sam's house and moved into Mickey's house. Eventually, they put on the addition for their expanding family. Their firstborn was a beautiful girl named Mary. Two years later, twin boys were born. They named the boys' Alan and Ellis, the last names of Scotty, Gage, and Neil. They picked the names; Mary, Alan, and Ellis for people who were part of starting their dream!

Sam became the head nurse at the hospital. Eventually, she moved into administration in order to spend more time with her family. Mickey continued to teach and coach wrestling. His wrestling program became one of the best in the state. Mickey has written articles about motivation. He travels the country giving motivational speeches.

Mickey and Sam and their family spend much time at the cabin in the mountains. They want their children to appreciate nature and the beauty around them. In the winter, they built a "snowy family." Mr. and Mrs. Snowy, and a girl and two boy snowys!

Sam even made sure that Mickey had his apron, which read 'kiss the cook,' on it, like his dad's. Sam sure made good use of that apron!

Mickey and Sam Cassman continue to teach their children to follow their dreams. Mickey and Sam continue to Follow their Dream!

About the Author

Glenn Bateman is a retired physical education teacher, who wrestled in high school and college, before coaching high school wrestling for over 35 years. Coach Bateman brings to life many personal issues facing high school athletes, and how to deal with these issues. Glenn also has experienced personal losses in his life, allowing him to share emotional attachments.

Glenn Bateman spends his retired life, living in Central Florida. He lives happily with his fiancée, Michele and their boxer dog, Tyson. He is an active 74-year-old, playing softball, pickleball, golf and basketball.

Made in United States
North Haven, CT
21 June 2023

38050045R00117